THE SPENCER SISTERS' FORBIDDEN LOVES AND BROKEN HEARTS

A Seabrook Family Saga, Book Six

CHRISTINE DONOVAN

Copyright @ 2019 by Christine Donovan

THE SPENCER SISTERS' FORBIDDEN LOVES AND BROKEN HEARTS

ISBN: 978-1-7334987-2-2

Cover Design by Wicked Smart Designs

Edited by Judy Roth

Sign up for Christine's newsletter to be informed of new releases and to be eligible for special contests and prizes. You can sign up on Christine's website at http://www.christinedonovan.org/

❀ Created with Vellum

This book is dedicated to my wonderful, beautiful, intelligent and creative seven-year-old granddaughter, Olivia Christine Donovan. She lights up my days with her smile.

She asked me the other day if I will write a kids book with her. Perhaps my next endeavor will be co-writing a children's book with Olivia. Nothing could make me prouder or more excited!

I love you Olivia!

Thank you to my husband, Michael and my four sons, Shawn, Matt, Danny and Joey. My granddaughter, Olivia, who never fails to make me smile and keeps life real. As always, to my mother, Alberta Murray, my sister, Karen Gomer for always supporting me. To my RIRW friends, Carolyn Sullivan, Jeanne Paglio and Joanne Smart for their encouragement and friendship throughout the years.

CHAPTER ONE

August 1818

MISS MARY SPENCER COULD HARDLY BELIEVE HER GOOD fortune at having the Bow Street Runner, and the man of her fantasies, Mr. Smythe riding with Aunt Violet, her sister Elizabeth, and herself for the twelve hours it would take to get to Cliff House in Hastings, the summer residence of the Marquess of Amesbury. Well, Smythe wasn't actually occupying the coach with them but riding on horseback looking lethal with a sinister rifle across his lap and two pistols in his holster. She imagined he had knives stashed somewhere on his person where she couldn't see.

Her body vibrated with awareness and other things she didn't understand at the sight of him. If she were a criminal she would run the other way in utter fear of her life.

"Why do you have an odd expression on your face," her elder sister by one year, Liz, who recently decided to be called by her complete name, Elizabeth, asked, straining her neck to see out Mary's window. Her sister looked lovely in her navy blue traveling clothes with matching bonnet. While Mary's hair was light, Elizabeth's was dark, but they both shared the same blue eyes.

Mary leaned forward, trying to block her view. "I don't." With heat burning her cheeks she knew she would not be able to hide her feelings for Mr. Smythe from her rather astute sister.

Elizabeth smiled the smile she did when she knew Mary had a secret. "You may as well tell me because I won't stop pestering you until you do."

Mary closed her eyes and was thankful Aunt Violet, as she wanted to be called, appeared to be sleeping. Aunt Violet was their sister-in-law, Miranda's aunt, and traveling with them as their chaperon. Their brother, Mr. Stuart Spencer, Spencer to all his friends and his new wife, Miranda, would join them in five days' time. Unfortunately, Aunt Violet was still recovering from being kidnapped and attacked by her scoundrel of a husband in the spring. Her only concession to traveling with them was with the accompaniment of the runner. "It appears I find Mr. Smythe appealing." There, she'd said it and it didn't seem all that strange voicing it out loud.

"I knew it!" Elizabeth squealed, waking Violet up. Both girls remained silent until she nodded off again. Her head dropped forward at an odd angle, and she began to snore softly.

"How did you know?" Mary asked as she smoothed out her skirts, giving her hands something to do.

"Only you and I know about the night and day you nursed Mr. Smythe after his injury, when Miranda and Aunt Violet were kidnapped and everyone else was out looking for them. It wasn't hard to realize because you've been acting lovesick since Spencer mentioned he would be escorting us."

Mary placed her hands on her cheeks. "Dear heavens, do

you think Spencer noticed? I couldn't live with myself if I caused trouble between he and Mr. Smythe."

"You do realize our brother will never allow him to court you? Although we all admire the man and all he's done for us and our family and friends." Elizabeth stared out the window and sighed. "As much as our brother is indebted to the man, I still don't think he would find him a suitable match for you."

With a woeful sigh, Mary leaned back against the padded squabs, closed her eyes, and tried to ignore the ache in her chest and the tears stinging her eyes. "I know all this, but I can't help hoping and wishing. I daydream about him and he intrudes on my dreams at night. This behavior coming from me, the sensible sister. I've never done anything remotely outside proper decorum members of the *Beau Monde* are supposed to adhere to." She glanced at Elizabeth and half smiled. "Not like someone else I know. It's a wonder you haven't caused a scandal and found yourself married to someone nasty and appalling." Her eyes traveled back out the window, not really seeing anything. "Don't you dare tell anyone, especially our brother, but I think I'm in love with him."

This time when Elizabeth squealed, Violet opened her eyes. "I heard every word. And if you ask me, which you didn't, that man has saved many lives, including Miranda's and mine. One may think he is worthy. You never know until you speak with Spencer."

Violet had the sisters' attention completely.

"You may be surprised at your brother's feelings about Mr. Smythe. Now, if you girls don't mind, I'm going back to sleep so I can dream of my own handsome lover." She cleared her throat. "Oh dear, did I say lover...pardon...I mean handsome gentleman. And don't look at me like that. I'm only forty. Still young enough to live...and love."

"What about you and Amesbury," Mary asked Elizabeth

softly when Violet appeared to be sleeping for real this time and not pretending. "I know how your mind works, and if I'm not mistaken, if he hasn't declared himself by the end of our visit, you my dear, devious, over-imaginative sister, will do something shocking to force his suit." Mary sighed wistfully. She could never do anything shocking. Sometimes she wished she had a small portion of Elizabeth's courage.

Mary turned sideways on the bench, hoping to study her sister's facial expression. Alas, she remained with her head turned toward the window and kept silent. Her body barely twitching.

"I...I hope you won't cause a scandal. I know what it's like to love someone you may never marry." Although Elizabeth had a better chance of marrying Amesbury than Mary did Mr. Smythe, which made fighting back tears even more difficult the more she dreamed of her very own Bow Street Runner.

Would she dare put herself in a compromising situation to force Mr. Smythe to ask for her hand? She didn't believe herself capable of doing such a thing on purpose. Some would think her nursing him after his injury this past spring would have caused a scandal and ruined her. Good thing no one other than her sister knew.

"Have you thought about what happens...when a man..." Elizabeth whispered as she turned and looked at Mary, shocking her at what she'd hinted at. Mary had some knowledge of the marriage bed, but not all of it. Only what her imagination allowed or what she heard whispered in drawing rooms and at balls. Or from some ridiculous book she and Elizabeth once found in their brother's chambers. She knew it involved nakedness and letting one's husband do as he pleased. It was the doing as he pleased that confused her.

"I know little except for what we saw in that book." Mary spoke barely above a whisper so as not to disturb Violet. The last thing they needed was more embarrassment and questions from their newly appointed aunt.

Elizabeth sighed and frowned. "As do I. I know I act as if I know everything, but sadly I don't." Then her face glowed and her lips curved up into a secretive smile. "Amesbury kissed me once. My heart jumped inside my chest, my palms sweated so unladylike, and my brain tingled as well as the rest of my body." She paused and leaned back on the seat. "He used his tongue."

Mary gasped, her eyes widening, "Go on, please."

"First his lips pressed against mine. They were surprisingly soft and warm." The tip of her index finger touched her lips. "When I opened my mouth to breathe or gasp, I can't remember which, he slanted his head, pulled me closer using his hand at the small of my back and plunged his tongue into my mouth."

They both gasped in unison, then sighed.

"Shocked." Elizabeth continued. "There are no other words to describe it. Indeed, I had heard about kissing with tongues, I just never imagined refined people such as us partaking in something so shocking." Elizabeth paused, which had Mary on the edge of her seat.

"Please don't keep me in suspense. What happened next." Mary needed to know because if she couldn't marry her beloved Mr. Smythe she believed she would die an innocent spinster, never having been kissed properly. Living vicariously through her sister would be her only option. May as well start now.

"I twirled my tongue with his. Then it was over. It happened at the beginning of the Season. Sometimes I think I dreamed it. I want to feel that way again. Reckless and free and loved." Elizabeth closed her eyes and sighed deeply.

"You will."

"How do you know?" Her sister's wishful expression had Mary hopeful for her own situation.

"I just do. Besides, Amesbury has to marry and produce an heir. If he kissed you, he must have feelings for you. Why wouldn't he marry you? Do you think Mr. Smythe will kiss me someday?"

Elizabeth glanced at her, compassion evident in her blue eyes so like her own. "For his and your sake, I pray not. It wouldn't end well I'm afraid. You don't want to cause a scandal and have Spencer send you to the country to live out your days as a spinster. Or worse, he'd marry you to a widower with a score of children, and you'll spend your life raising someone else's chits. Besides, what would I do without you?"

Mary refused to believe her sister. If Spencer highly trusted and admired Smythe, why wasn't he good enough for her? She didn't care if she had to reside in a less desirable part of London. Even in a rundown tenement in St. Giles as long as she and Smythe were together. Smythe, good God she didn't even know his Christian name. Hopeless. Her life was hopeless.

While Mary daydreamed, Elizabeth leaned against her and dozed. She, however, stared wide-eyed out the window hoping for a glimpse of Smythe. When he didn't enter her range of vision she leaned back, pulled the blanket resting on her lap up to her chin, and closed her tired eyes. Her mind raced for a time until sleep took over and she had peace.

EVER SINCE THEY hit the outskirts of London, Mr. Robert Smythe, Bow Street Runner, had fidgeted in his saddle as a familiar awareness prickled up and down his spine. He'd always had a perceptive intuition. It kept him and his men alive. Not to mention keeping himself safe when he'd lived on the streets as a young lad. But bloody hell, not now.

Spencer had hired him to keep the ladies safe, and he would do anything to accomplish the task. Even give his life without a moment's hesitation. As they continued down a normally well-traveled road—strange they were the only carriage within sight—suspicions came and went, keeping him on high alert. His intense eyes scanned the area continually but came up empty until up ahead dark thunderous clouds threatened their otherwise uneventful journey.

By late afternoon Smythe decided to make an unexpected stop at the Horse and Pony Inn for the night. He didn't mind pushing through the storm, but the horses were skittish and the roads turning impassable. After eating an early dinner, Robert saw to it the three ladies were locked in one room together and traipsed to the barn to bed down with the driver and one outrider. The other outrider he sent ahead to Cliff House to advise Lord Amesbury of their change in plans. Smythe proceeded to toss and turn until he gave up on sleep, made his way back inside the inn, and sat down with his back leaning up against the door of the room the ladies occupied. No one would get in or out without going through him.

Eventually he nodded off and dreamed about one of the ladies inside...Mary. A lady so above his station he had to be daft in the head to conceive of ever being with her in the way he wanted. Well, he decided he was indeed daft in the head because he couldn't imagine not seeing her or worse, seeing her married to some dandy who didn't know his arse from his elbow.

Near disasters had a habit of wreaking havoc on her family and friends. He'd been employed quite a few times in the past two years by the lot of them. The odds of him being hired in the future and being forced to watch Mary interact with the man she married was a plausible scenario.

Confound it, he was doomed to a life devoid of love. He knew in his heart he would never marry or love another. Mary, only Mary. Spending twenty-four hours in her presence during his convalescence from a knife wound several months ago was all it took. He'd fallen fast and hard and knew he'd never recover or regain his heart back.

In the morning, the outrider Smythe had sent ahead to Hastings arrived back at the inn and advised Smythe that the roads were still impassible. The sun shined brightly, hopefully soaking up the extensive puddles so they could leave in the afternoon. Which they did.

At three, Smythe went to the barn and assisted the driver and outriders in readying the coach for the five hours they had left to travel. The innkeeper's wife supplied food enough for their travels, and he stored the large basket inside the boot. He'd skipped the midday meal, and his stomach growled at the divine smells coming from the basket.

Just then he heard voices and his eyes were riveted on Mary. Her dark green traveling clothes hugged her lush figure and made her eyes look more green than her normal blue. Her light hair was tucked up inside a small hat, and he'd dreamed of it often enough that he could envision the silky strands running through his fingers and tickling his naked chest.

Before he realized what he intended to do, he swept past the driver, opened the coach door, dropped down the steps, and helped first Lady Violet, then Miss Elizabeth inside. When it came to Mary, their eyes locked as their gloved hands connected. A shy smile crossed her lips then she lowered her lashes and disappeared inside the coach. All safe and sound from his wicked thoughts. Once again he realized how doomed his life was.

He expected them to arrive at Cliff House by nightfall if they didn't make many stops or encounter washed out roads.

The weather turned as they progressed toward Hastings. Gray skies threatened and wind howled, forcing Robert to pull the brim of his hat down low and the collar of his riding jacket up. He prayed they didn't ride into a storm again, and the weather improved soon. However, light fog rolled in and they were forced to slow the horses. They couldn't risk an accident, not with the roads muddy and large puddles still here and there.

Regrettably, they did ride into a storm, not the one Robert thought, but the one he was hired to avoid. *Highwaymen*. Horses' hooves off in the distance, getting closer by the second, pounded inside Robert's ears. Four horses to be exact. Before they saw him he kicked his horse and entered the surrounding woods. He should've been more alert and not been daydreaming about Mary. If his lack of attention caused anyone to be hurt, or worse, he would never forgive himself.

Four men with bandanas covering the lower half of their faces approached with guns drawn. Two on each side of the coach. Their speed and horses, not to mention the muddy road, were no match for the coach so the driver didn't even try to outrun them.

The riders didn't see Robert yet. He knew he had seconds to act. As the reins were taken from the driver and the carriage wheels came to a sudden stop he heard what sounded like Violet scream. He had to detach himself from the scene and the people, especially Mary, and go into protector mode.

Before the men had a chance to get the women out of the coach, he picked off the closet to the door with his riffle. No time to reload, he withdrew both pistols from his gun belt and started shooting just as bullets flew toward him. One grazed his shoulder, he ignored it. Better him than anyone else in their riding party. The outriders were both armed and shot back as well.

After what seemed like hours, but in reality only seconds

went by, two men rode off into the forest leaving two men dead on the ground, their horses having followed the men into the woods.

As the door to the coach started to open Robert yelled, "Stay inside and whatever you do, don't look outside."

The two outriders and Robert dragged the dead men into the woods and left them. He made a mental note of what the other men looked like and what type of mounts they rode. Once in Hastings he would send word to his office, and with any luck the offenders would be captured before they attacked anyone else. His body shuttered. He'd been lucky. If he hadn't had time to hide in the edge of the forest, God only knew what would've happened. Most likely they were looking for coin and jewels. But highwaymen had been known to kidnap and rape. His insides coiled up tight, and he felt sick knowing it would have been his fault.

He dismounted, ignoring the fiery pain radiating from his shoulder and down his entire right side. It was a damn good thing he could shoot equally well with both hands. He opened the door and stepped inside the coach to assure himself all were unharmed and safe and to appease his run-a-way heart, which had lodged itself inside his throat. He made his apologizes as he sat next to Violet. He was too bloody tall to stand inside the coach. His eyes found Mary first, wide-eyed with fright, which tortured his insides even more.

"They are gone. I don't expect any more trouble. Please stay inside, and we will get you safely to Cliff House by nightfall."

"Mr. Smythe," Miss Elizabeth interrupted. "You are bleeding."

"Yes, I know. A bullet grazed my shoulder."

"No. I mean your side."

His hand went to his side and sure enough it made

contact with warm blood. He'd felt when the bullet hit his shoulder, but not that one.

"Please stay seated and let me bandage your wound," Mary said, looking pale and unsteady.

Elizabeth banged on the trapdoor to get the attention of the driver. He lifted it up. "Please tie Mr. Smythe's horse to the carriage, he has been wounded, and then get us to Cliff House as fast as you can.

"Only need a bandage and I can go back to my horse. I need to keep watch in case..."

Violet cried out, "I thought you said we shouldn't have any more trouble."

Damn, he should've kept his mouth shut. "It's just a precaution." He could tell neither of the three believed him. But hell, he didn't expect them to come back. Robbers liked easy conquests. Not ones where they were shot at and killed.

Robert found himself at the mercy of the three ladies instead of the other way around. Mary assisted him in removing his riding jacket and waistcoat. In his dreams this was not how it happened.

Now what? Were they honestly going to remove his shirt? Which he had to admit had two large stains of blood, one spreading more rapidly than the other.

"Mr. Smythe," Mary began, "I realize this is most improper, but your shirt must be removed so I may see the extent of your injuries and to bind them up." As she finished speaking she rummaged through a bag and pulled out a lady's undergarment.

Bloody bugger, she planned to bind his wounds with her unmentionables. If he wasn't already in pain from two gunshot wounds, he'd be in pain somewhere else. Mr. Spencer was going to have his hide for this. He tried to keep his shirt on, but he was no match against three stubborn ladies.

Several hands tried to help him with his shirt and he pushed them away. "I can do it myself." He grumbled.

He loosened the top of his shirt and used his good arm to pull it over his head. He tried not to hiss, however, his shirt clung to his injuries and removing it hurt like hell. Once he managed to remove it, he inhaled and exhaled several times as he sat back—only to spring forward in agony, shutting his eyes against the pain and sudden spots invading his vision. It would be a cold day in hell before he passed out in front of Mary. Speaking of Mary, her soothing, concerned voice reached out to him.

"May I inspect your wounds?"

It brought back memories of the night she watched over him. A night which changed the trajectory of his life forever.

"Yes," he answered. He kept his eyes closed and concentrated on her gentle hands using a cloth to wipe away the blood and not the pain burning inside his body.

"Your shoulder looks good. The bullet did only nick it. I'm still going to bandage it though." Tender, loving hands and a calming voice apologized if she hurt him in anyway, lulled him away from his pain.

"Your side is bleeding quite profusely. I can't tell if the bullet is still inside you or not...oh...the scar from your knife wound healed nicely though." The two other occupants of the carriage gasped. Mary ignored them.

"Let me," he said as he sucked in air, leaned forward and felt around his back. Lucky for him he found the exit wound. With any luck it didn't hit any vital organs. If it did things wouldn't turn out well for him. Or the ladies, as he'd be dead within the hour.

"The bullet's out. Wrap me up please. I'll be fine." His eyes opened and his jaw dropped. Mary, lovely Mary had tears in her soft blue eyes. Never did he think she looked more beautiful.

WHEN THE HORRIBLE men had stopped their coach and yelled orders for the driver to stop, Mary watched Violet closely, expecting her to faint. One really could not blame her after her husband, Mr. Baker, absconded with her then did unspeakable things to her. Somehow she'd managed to remain calm, except for one loud scream.

When Smythe entered the carriage and Mary's eyes fell on the blood seeping across his waistcoat and shirt, she'd almost fainted. She'd dug her nails into the palms of her hands to keep her mind clear. The poor man got shot twice protecting them. The thought of him dying had her heart in tatters. It would not come to fruition. She would not let him die. Even if nothing ever came of the feelings she possessed for him, she still wouldn't let him die.

As she helped him strip off his clothes, her face burned with embarrassment at seeing his muscular chest sprinkled with brown hair. Her virgin eyes had never seen such a sight. Not even when she'd nursed him after he received a stab wound. He'd been clothed in a nightshirt. All she'd done was help him fight the infection and fever.

She'd never even seen her brother without a shirt on. If it wasn't for the blood marring his chest and shoulder and the bullet wounds, she may have looked her fill. Instead, she did all she could to stop the blood, save his life, and make him comfortable. All three proved difficult in a fast moving carriage on rutted, muddy country roads.

London would be a far worse place without the famed Bow Street Runner keeping the streets safe. Or at the very least, trying to keep them safe. One man could only do so much when an army was needed.

CHAPTER TWO

KNOWING ELIZABETH WOULD BE ARRIVING AT ANY TIME, Edward Worthington, Marquess of Amesbury, paced back and force in the green drawing room. Horrible scenarios raced through his over-imaginative mind. He couldn't conceive what was keeping them. Except he could and none of the imagines were good. Two outriders, one driver, and Smythe should keep them safe. Smythe *would* keep them safe. The man never let any of them in their circle of friends down. Not that Edward had ever personally hired the runner, but he'd seen him in action aplenty. If his family still lived he'd trust Smythe with their lives. Damn, thinking of his parents and sister still caused his heart to break each and every time, which was less often these days, and that made him sad and cross at the same time.

Wallowing in a past he could never change would not help ease his concern. For some unfortunate reason, danger had followed his friends like a dark stormy cloud the past two years. With his heart pounding against his chest he prayed not this time. The woman he hoped to marry occupied the carriage, and he wouldn't know what would become of him if something terrible should befall her. Edward's hands itched to yank at his hair, snapping him out of his morbid thoughts, as he spotted a faint light in the distance moving slowly along. He ran to the front door past the startled doorman, flung open the heavy wooden door and leaped the four stairs at once, landing just as the carriage came to a quick halt.

"Greetings milord," the driver said as he climbed down from his perch. "We've had a wee bit of trouble. The ladies are safe and unharmed but Mr. Smythe was shot twice."

Edward yanked the door open and flipped down the stairs before the coachman landed on solid ground. Hearing the driver's words and seeing Smythe struggle out of the coach refusing help had him barking orders, "Peabody, send one of the under footman for Doctor Connolly and tell him not to return without the good doctor."

Once Smythe exited safety, Edward assisted the ladies down, barely acknowledging them since he knew they were unarmed and there would be time to speak to them once Smythe was settled. Worried for Smythe's safety as he was, he looked at the sudden flutter of activity and barked, "Where is Mrs. Glendale?"

A middle aged, plump woman answered, "Right here, milord."

"Please have clean towels, hot water, bandages, and anything else you can think of brought to Mr. Smythe's chamber."

"Oh...and also...please escort the ladies to their rooms." As Edward turned to assist Smythe up the stairs his eyes settled on Elizabeth long enough for him to be assured she appeared unharmed. Bloody hell, if anything happened to her he would never forgive himself, not to mention he'd be crushed. One could only handle so much loss in life before one became permanently damaged. Heart and soul.

Once inside the chambers prepared for Smythe, Edward

was so very thankful his housekeeper's gentle, competent hands took care of the injured runner.

When Dr. Connolly arrived harried and carrying an ancient carpet bag, Edward sighed with relief. He dropped into a chair across the room facing the recently stoked fireplace. It was his opinion, no finer doctor existed anywhere in England. Smythe was in capable hands.

Staring into the flames for what seemed forever, Edward tried not to let his imagination run wild. What was taking the doctor so long? Unease and worry prickled his skin and he shivered.

"Lord Amesbury, may I have a word with you?"

As he approached the physician at Smythe's bedside, he found the runner sleeping and was grateful he still lived. Since when had the roads between London and Hastings become so dangerous? Since all of London's elite decided Hastings was the place to be this summer. Highwaymen knew riches were for the pickings.

"How is he?" Edward asked cautiously.

"He lost a lot of blood, but the man is lucky. The bullets pierced nothing vital. If infection does not set in, he'll make a full recovery. With the blood loss he will be weak for some time. However, he's a young and healthy man. It won't take long for his strength to be restored." The doctor put several small glass bottles on the table next to the bed. Then packed up his bag. "I left laudanum to take for pain and to help him sleep. Give it to him every four hours. I will stop by tomorrow. Goodnight your lordship."

Sweat broke out on Edward's brow. Tremors began in his hands and spread like the London fire of 1666 throughout his body. Laudanum—opium—he couldn't be near the stuff. Suddenly realizing Mrs. Glendale still occupied the room he somehow managed to mumble, "Please watch over our patient and administer his medicine."

Without waiting for a reply, he flew out of the room, careful not to slam the door when he exited. Leaning forward, his hands resting on his thighs, he breathed in and out deeply many times, fighting the sickness inside his stomach. When he heard her soft voice he realized he wasn't alone in the hallway.

"Amesbury, is he...is he dead?" Elizabeth cried out.

It took him a moment to comprehend the question as his ears rang from the pounding of his blood running wild. "What? No. Smythe is expected to recover."

"Oh. Thank God. Mary would be heartbroken if he died."

He didn't need to look to know she approached him and tentatively placed a warm hand on his upper arm. "Are you unwell?"

The concern in her voice almost broke him. He didn't deserve Elizabeth's compassion. Not after the things he'd done. The monster he'd become after his family's death. The monster, he'd realized only moments ago, still lived inside him. He was vile and dirty. She was pure and everything virtuous.

"Amesbury?" More worry in her voice as her fingers curled tightly around his arm.

What to say? He didn't know how to answer her. "Yes. Everything is well. Please except my apologies if I caused you any undue concern." He inhaled and exhaled. "Should you not go to Mary and give her the good news?"

Startled, she withdrew her hand and answered softly, "Yes."

The touch of her hand on his forearm had soothed him and he missed the contact immediately. He truly didn't wish for her to leave him, but she had to before he had another breakdown in front of her. Edward hurried down the stairs and made his way to his study where he had a full bottle of Scotch whiskey waiting for him.

WITH ALL THE chaos that ensued upon their arrival to Cliff House, Miss Elizabeth Spencer barely got a glimpse of Amesbury before he disappeared inside Smythe's chamber for what seemed to be hours.

The whole entire carriage ride—through the fog, deep jarring ruts in the country roads, the highwaymen and Smythe's wounds—she'd thought of Amesbury. Knowing the man she loved resided at the end of her travels kept her calm.

She hadn't known what to expect when she arrived, but it wasn't what transpired. Of course, when she daydreamed about arriving Smythe wasn't injured. In her dreams Amesbury welcomed their coach, helped her down and immediately pulled her into his strong arms and kissed her senseless, not caring who witnessed his declaration of love. And clearly he would never kiss her in public without declaring himself afterwards. It would be scandalous. But she didn't care. Too bad daydreams never came true.

Indeed, in her dreams Mr. Smythe's life wasn't in peril. She said a silent prayer the doctor was right in believing Mr. Smythe would recover. If he didn't get well many of her friends and family members, most especially Mary, would mourn the runner's death if it came to that horrible ending. *He was...is...a good man.* She hoped Spencer agreed, she knew he did, but would he think him worthy of Mary?

Since spending two days traveling in Mary and Smythe's company, there was no doubt in her mind he was as drawn to Mary as she to him. When Smythe thought no one watched he looked at her with eyes gone soft and wanting. Would Amesbury ever look at her the same way? Perhaps he had but she'd not witnessed it. If he had, it would be a look she'd never forget.

If he didn't declare himself during her visit, she would be

having a third Season next year. A third? How extremely mortifying. Mary would be experiencing her second. Still time for Mary. If after Elizabeth's third Season, she failed to catch a husband, she would be considered a failure and well on her way to spinsterhood. How utterly absurd. She had many good years ahead of her.

Why, look at her sister-in-law, Miranda? She'd married her brother just recently, and she was nine and twenty and never previously married.

Although Spencer asked for her hand in marriage during her first Season, Miranda's father refused because of the scandal surrounding their cousin, the Earl of Bridgeton, who'd been accused of murdering his brother and sister-in-law, which was absurd. Miranda thought he never asked and Spencer was told by her father that she never wanted to see him again. How extremely sad.

Twelve years later, they encountered each other again. Neither of them having married, the same emotional, loving feelings swept them away and they finally married. It made her believe anything between her and Amesbury was possible.

When they'd arrived at Cliff House, a distraught Mary was shown to her room by a kindly maid. Violet retired to her room, not looking her best, which left Elizabeth waiting outside Smythe's room in the long shadowy hallway alone. When finally, the door opened and the doctor exited, she tried to speak to him. He mumbled, "Speak to Lord Amesbury."

More time waiting, her fingernails were a mess as she chewed them off one by one, causing one of them to bleed. She sucked on it, hoping to get it to stop when the door opened and closed again. It was the man of her dreams. Or at least she thought it was. If his expression was any indication, something terrible was amiss. His face looked white as a newly laundered sheet. He leaned forward, gripping his thighs with his hands while his body convulsed.

Having never seen any man show such emotion, she wondered what to do. Obviously he'd not seen her and believed he was alone. What to do? She did what came naturally to her. She spoke in soothing tones and curled her hand around his upper arm. When really what she wanted to do was wrap her arms around him and bury her head in the crook of his neck and tell him all would be well. But would it? Not if Smythe was dead. Dear God, please let him be alive.

"Amesbury is he...is he dead?"

When Amesbury answered and said Smythe would heal, Elizabeth almost collapsed to the floor in relief. Relief for Mary. And then he all but dismissed her and stumbled away down the dreary hallway leaving her with tears burning her eyes and her heart crushed. Once his figure was no longer in sight and his boots didn't make thumping noises, she stood tall, wiped her eyes and silently made her way to her sister's room.

After one knock on the door, Mary flung it opened—if it wasn't such a heavy wooden door Elizabeth thought it might have flown off the hinges—looking frightful. Her eyes were red-rimmed and swollen, her hair wet and tangled. A panicked expression was plastered on her splotchy face. A face usually calm and radiantly beautiful. Mary's skin so pale in color didn't look attractive when she cried.

"The doctor said he will recover," Elizabeth blurted out before her sister had a brain bleed or something equally awful. Elizabeth entered the room, shut the door, and pulled her sister into her arms. "Shhhh, there, there. He's going to live. I'm quite convinced you can visit him tomorrow, first thing in the morning."

"D...Do you think so?"

"Yes. Come to bed. I'll sit with you until you fall asleep. I know how you hate sleeping alone in strange houses."

Mary climbed in the bed and Elizabeth helped pull the coverlet up to her chin. "Thank you," Mary murmured."

"Try to relax, sleep, and dream about your handsome Mr. Smythe when he is robust and healthy." After a time, she knew Mary slept. Her breathing evened out, and she made soft snoring sounds. Feeling sleepy herself after their travels and the dreadful attack and not wanting to be alone, she decided to join Mary in bed. She removed her traveling clothes and stays, slid beneath the covers in her chemise and joined her sister in sleep, dreaming about her own handsome man. Only in her dream Amesbury appeared unwell. Pale, shaky, weak, and agitated.

EDWARD TOSSED around from side to side on his bed. Switching from lying on his stomach to his back. Nothing helped. All he saw in his mind's eye was the brown glass vile beside Smythe's bed.

Laudanum, opium, whatever one chose to name it, was his weakness in life and once his undoing. Before he knew what he planned, his legs slid to the cool rug covering the wooden floors, and he looked down and shook his head. He veritably could not traipse through his home in only his nightshirt. Entering his dressing room, he donned a navy silk banyan, tying the sash around his waist tightly. Plucking an oil lamp from his bedside table, and with the aid of his cane as his legs were quite numb and unsteady, he quietly opened his bedchamber door, glad he had ordered all the doors oiled recently, and he shuffled silently down the hallway to Smythe's room.

Before opening the door, Edward knocked gently. Hearing

no response, he opened it a crack, peered inside, grateful a lamp illuminated the room. A sigh of relief escaped his lungs at finding the room empty of people except for Smythe. Making his way inside, it wasn't lost on him he was sneaking around in his own home. Swearing at himself, he shut the door and stood looking down at Smythe, who appeared to be in a drug induced sleep.

One Edward wanted to experience. He missed opium. The feeling of not caring, not remembering the tragic, bloody night he lost both his parents and his younger sister who had her entire life ahead of her snuffed out in a reckless carriage accident. The driver and the outriders had imbibed too much spirits.

His parents and sister died for their servants' stupidity. For years he wished he'd died alongside them. Life alone proved unbearable at times. In the early years and then later, Wentworth and Myles saved him.

First they helped him recover from a broken back and terrible grief. Years later, with encouragement and support, they saved him from the poison currently taking up residence on Smythe's night table.

The pull toward the drug was a powerful one. Without thought, he moved to the small mahogany table and with trembling hands, picked up the vile and removed the stopper. The potent scent wafted up his nostrils and had him frozen in place—the smell as familiar to himself as his own scent.

Abruptly, something in the universe shifted. Saliva filled his mouth, rolled down his chin and neck. Tears filled his eyes and streaked down his cheeks. His body convulsed violently, forcing his fingers to release the drug and send it tumbling to the floor, spilling the contents on the carpet, making the powerful smell even stronger. Moments later he found himself on all fours fighting not to vomit. "Easy, take one deep breath at a time." Sounded reasonable saying it out loud, except breathing deeply only brought the laudanum scent stronger inside his nostrils.

"Amesbury, are you unwell?" Hadn't she asked the very thing earlier? The concerned voice of the woman he believed he loved but didn't deserve shocked him. He used his banyan sleeve to wipe his face. He couldn't have Elizabeth seeing him in such a state.

He needed time with Elizabeth alone to know if he loved her, but know couldn't be a worse time. And really, how did one know if they were in love if they'd never been? If not love, in the very least, would they suit? These things he needed to know before he asked Spencer for her hand. If the drool wasn't bad enough, now sweat broke out on his brow at the thought of marriage. Promising to love someone until death.

Death.

There was a time Edward believed he would never marry or have heirs. The pain of losing them would be unbearable. Something he knew he wouldn't survive. More sweat, this time dripping down the side of his face.

Death. It had ruled his life for so long.

Edward had never believed his lifelong friend, the Duke of Wentworth, would marry, find love and have a family after what his father had done. The previous duke had squandered the family fortune on mistresses and gambling and drank himself to death. But Wentworth did. He married a lovely American, Emma. His friend was beyond happy and in love.

Same for the Earl of Northborough, whom everyone referred to as Myles. He married Wentworth's sister Bella after death and sickness plagued him and his family. Not to mention, being poisoned by his cousin, the next in line to inherit.

So after all that adversity, they were happy and content in marriage. Why not him? That question haunted Edward.

After what he'd done to himself and his continued daily struggles, what right did he have to bring Elizabeth into his nightmares. Only a selfish bastard would.

If only...

"Amesbury, I asked if you are unwell?" The concern in her voice caused guilt to consume him.

"I came to check on Smythe and accidently knocked over a vile of Laudanum. How clumsy of me." As he spoke he shoved his cane beneath Smythe's bed. Sheer determination would keep him from using it.

"Let me help you."

"No." He'd spoken more harshly than intended by the shock and hurt he glimpsed on her face in the low candle-light. "Forgive me. I can manage on my own." His trembling fingers put the stopper back on the vile to save whatever medicine was left inside. He climbed to his feet, ignoring the slice of pain radiating up both his legs and up his spine. After placing the vile on the nightstand he pivoted around and came face to face with Elizabeth. His lungs failed him and he gasped.

Dressed only in a thin, white chemise with a wrap draped loosely across her shoulders, she was breathtakingly beautiful. He would never trust himself if she came closer.

Years. It had been years since he bedded a woman. Mistresses and whores were never his style. And since he didn't believe in deflowering innocents, well, that left him with widows. Suffice it to say, before Wentworth married Emma, he had that market of woman satisfied.

Edward had spent one year betrothed to Lady Elizabeth Duncan, otherwise addressed as Lady Beth. Thankfully after a year her father broke the marriage contract. Wentworth had gone to the man and explained how Edward was ill and would make his daughter miserable. The man believed him, thank God. Happy and free once again, except Edward wanted the woman in the room with him more than he wanted air to breathe. Or thankfully, more than opium. He cringed at the thought of being an opium eater again. Or visiting the Red Poppy with all the other opium eaters of the *ton* and doing despicable things.

Tonight he'd come close, very close. Too close in his opinion.

"Excuse my forwardness," Elizabeth said quietly, "you appear troubled by something. I've been told I'm a good listener. Would you care to go somewhere and talk?"

Bloody hell, did she know what she asked of him? If they went somewhere private and were found out she would be ruined. Although who would say anything? Not his servants, not Violet, Mary, or Smythe.

"The library is my favorite place at this hour." Had those words come from him?

Once inside the room, he stoked the embers in the fireplace, added several logs until a flame sputtered to life. Elizabeth had chosen to sit on the comfortable settee and patted the seat next to her.

If he joined her, he didn't know if he could keep his hands to himself. His body ignored his mind because before he knew it, he sat down beside her, leaving several inches between them.

"Go ahead and unburden yourself. Nothing discussed leaves this room."

He turned his head and looked at her in horror.

"Forgive me. That sounded callous and unfeeling when to tell the truth my heart is hurting for the pain you seem to be experiencing. I want to wrap my arms around you until all is well."

She appeared most sincere. Her eyes compassionate and misty as though tears would drip from them at any moment.

For the first time in hours, his heart eased and he felt

compelled to confide in her something only his two closest friends knew. Although even they didn't know all.

However, a part of him was petrified she would go running to Spencer when she heard all the secrets of his past. What would the man think of him then?

"Would you...could you hold me?" He shocked himself to hear the words escape from his lips, nevertheless they did, and there was no going back now. Nor did he want to. If he disgusted her, better to find out now.

"Place your head on my lap. Get comfortable and relax. I won't let you fall."

So he did as she suggested. It was cramped as he curled on his side, his knees bent and his head pillowed in Elizabeth's soft lap. The first thing he noticed was her scent. He inhaled the fresh, clean scent like wildflowers blowing in the breeze. Her hand caressing his hair soothed him, and he never wanted her to stop. Scandalous as their behavior was, he couldn't bring himself to leave his current position.

It'd been years since he slept through the night because of his nightmares and constant pain, which worsened in the evening hours. Although he had a feeling if he closed his eyes now, he'd fall into a deep slumber.

"I imagine you know my parents and sister perished in a carriage accident coming home late one night from visiting family friends in the country." The rise and fall of her breathing was a balm to his soul.

"Yes. I was young. But I remember it well. I'm so sorry."

"Thank you," he whispered. His throat clogged with unwanted tears. Clearing it, he forged on before he lost his nerve. "I entered the carriage last. I'd noticed the driver and outriders appeared in their cups."

Elizabeth gasped and her hand stilled.

"I don't know why I ignored it and didn't say something to my father." He groaned loudly. "I'm the reason they're dead. All of them. When the carriage rolled down the embankment it crushed everyone but Jane and I. The screams as the coach rolled still echo in my dreams until nothing but silence prevails." Tears ran down his cheeks onto Elizabeth's lap, wetting her chemise, but he couldn't help it. His heart shattered all over again. "I lay on the ground on my back at an odd angle. I couldn't move as I'd broken it. My sister lay only several feet away, much like me.

"It took all my strength and concentration to reach out to her. Jane did likewise. Inches kept our hands from touching. I felt helpless to help her. She cried out, 'Help me Edward. I can't feel my body.' Her eyes glowed from the light of the full moon—her tears illuminating them more. She had the prettiest amber eyes. I lay their struggling to reach her hand to no avail. And I watched in horror, as ever so slowly, life extinguished from her eyes and she took her last breath. I stared into her lifeless eyes for what seemed an eternity until help came in the form of a local farmer and his wife. Jane's eyes are the last thing I see when I fall asleep at night. If I'm able to sleep at all."

Swinging his legs off the settee, Edward bolted up, dropped his face into his hands and cried. He couldn't stop the emotions from bombarding his senses. He'd never really let himself mourn his family. His entire being ached from his emotional purge. Perhaps someday he'd feel better, having shared his guilt. But not now. Now he didn't know what he felt except drained. Emotionally and physically drained and embarrassed for Elizabeth seeing him that way.

CHAPTER THREE

ELIZABETH'S HEART BLED FOR AMESBURY. SHE'D NEVER SEEN a grown man cry, and she didn't know what to do. So she did what she'd do for her sister. She wrapped her arms around him and murmured, "There, there, all will be well, you'll see." She placed kisses on the top of his head as she hugged him to her chest. "Shhh, I know it appears hopeless, but you are a strong man. Your family doesn't blame you."

He lifted his head and looked directly into her eyes and her heart broke. Hopeful, red-rimmed watery eyes looked into hers for answers. If she hadn't loved him already, she would now. "How do you know? Do you talk to the dead?"

Talk to the dead? Not likely.

"No. But they loved you. Still love you. They wouldn't want you to live with the guilt, when the truth is, it was a terrible accident. And I like to believe when people die, it's because God is calling them home to His side."

He pushed her away suddenly, stood and paced, off balance, back and forth on the rug centered in front of the hearth. He ran his hands, none too gently through his hair, almost as though he wished to tear the strands out. "I've done unspeakable things in the years since. I don't deserve, nor want your pity."

Unspeakable things? Elizabeth didn't dare dwell on what constituted *unspeakable*.

When he stopped pacing and looked directly at her, his eyes were guarded. Back to hiding his guilt and secrets. Guilt and secrets tearing him apart little by little. How had she never noticed the turmoil, self-hatred, and suffering he dealt with on a daily basis? Simple. He hid it well. No one who knew him outside of this home would ever reconcile this man here tonight with the impeccable marquess who prowled drawing rooms, clubs, and balls on a nightly basis.

Something needed to change, though, because she'd set her sights on him. She loved him. What better time than now, to show him that his past didn't change her feelings for him. Only one small problem? Since she came out the previous Season, she'd played at being knowledgeable where men were concerned, shocking her family with some of her words and behavior, just shy of being ruinous. When truth be told, besides kissing Amesbury once, she knew nothing about seduction or what a man wanted. Everything she knew came from a sex manual she'd found in Spencer's room many years ago. A book with crude drawings.

There hadn't been much in the book she could imagine doing. She went with instinct. Elizabeth walked up behind him, circled her arms around his waist and rested her cheek on his back between his shoulder blades. It was as far as she reached. Amesbury stood nearly a foot taller than her.

When her arms first wrapped around him, his entire body tensed. When her cheek pressed softly against his back, his tension intensified. Then slowly, ever so slowly, muscle by muscle, tendon after tendon eased. His heart which beat rapidly against her ear also calmed.

"Thank you," he said

"For what?"

"For ignoring the fact I behaved deplorably. Not at all like the marquess and gentleman I'm supposed to be."

Confused, she asked, "Surely you jest? You are a marquess and a gentleman to the core of your being. Don't ever think otherwise. I don't, neither does anyone else."

"Yes. Well." He placed his large hands on top of hers, and warmth settled nicely inside her heart. "Sometimes I've disregarded my morals and...We can speak about that another time." He turned toward her, his arms around her back and rested his cheek on the top of her head. "After your travels and the excitement you endured you need your rest. Allow me to escort you to your chamber."

She didn't want to leave the library. She'd never been this close physically and emotionally with Amesbury, and pray tell, she didn't want it to end. Elizabeth's insides quaked at the thought of breaking the connection with him. It may be all she ever received from him. She loved him, and she believed he cared for her, but would anything come from it? After all, he'd been betrothed once for a whole year and the marriage never took place. Something she'd always pondered about. Indeed, she was elated the nuptials never took place, but still...she wondered.

He'd been stricken with a mysterious illness, which still remained a mystery. During that time Lady Beth's father ended the betrothal under baffling circumstances. Elizabeth wanted to know what happened so if by some miracle they become affianced, it wouldn't have the same outcome. She swallowed her gasp at realizing for the first time they shared the same name. Would fate be cruel a second time? No, she refused to believe any such thing.

Tilting her head up, she looked at the man holding her. If he truly looked into her eyes he'd see love and longing. A love so deep she believed she'd never be whole if he didn't return it. A longing so extreme even she didn't understand all she longed for.

His Adams apple bobbed as he swallowed hard and loud, fascinating her. "We should..." he said in a deep baritone.

Suddenly parched, her tongue darted out and slid across her lips.

He groaned.

She whispered, "I agree, we should."

His eyes flickered from her lips to her eyes and back, causing her body to sway closer and tingles to dance up her spine.

"Should what?" he murmured.

As the air expelled from her lungs, she said the word fast before she lost her nerve, "Kiss."

A KISS? What harm could one little kiss cause? Edward new the moment his lips came in contact with hers, control would vanish for him. As he held her soft, pliant body, which trembled in his arms now, he knew he had to taste her. He was a man being offered a kiss by the woman he cared for most in his life, even if he never admitted it to anyone, much less her. How could he refuse her request for a kiss? He would do anything to never see disappointment on her face.

Her full, newly moist, pink lips slightly parted, tempted him, so he did what came natural. He dropped his head and captured her mouth. A mewing sound escaped her. He splayed his hand on the small of her back and pulled her close, so their bodies touched intimately where it mattered most. Neither of their scant clothing provided much of a barrier. His hips were forward, his arousal making full contact with her lower stomach, and he groaned with need. A need so deep within his soul, it frightened him.

Tilting his head for better access, he thrust his tongue inside her warm mouth. It traveled to unexplored places and crevices, her hands moved to his hair and held on as she swirled her tongue with his and became an avid participant in the mating of their mouths.

Again her body trembled and little sighs and moans came here and there when she breathed. Her hands moved from his hair down his back. Tentatively they caressed side to side and up and down, fueling his lust he could not get release from. Not with Elizabeth. Not unless they wed. When they wed. *Wed?*

Disconnecting from her emotionally and physically, he stepped back twice, took a deep shaky breath, and let it out. Ignoring her parted, swollen lips, her glazed eyes, he spoke. "I'll see you to your room." It amazed him the words came out without relaying all the emotions warring inside him.

She blinked, her eyes focusing, and she frowned. He waited several moments for her to speak. "Thank you."

When they reached the door to her chamber, he bent down and placed a chaste kiss on her forehead. "Sleep well."

Once inside his rooms, he poured himself a brandy and sat by the warm hearth. What was he to do about Elizabeth? If the world were a perfect, happy place he would marry her in a second and produce heirs. She would say yes if he asked. He could see it in her lovely blue eyes. He may as well admit to himself that he did indeed love her. So why did his heart ache so? Why, after dealing with his past issues of family loss, guilt that he lived with and his addiction to opium, did he suddenly feel unsettled and on the verge of out of control behavior. He'd been getting better. Dealing with all his problems with a clear head. Except fear. Fear that Spencer, when he found out the truth of his past, would refuse to allow Elizabeth and he to wed. Fear as an emotion, was the one that terrorized him now. He'd not experienced this depth of fear in the past not since the carriage accident. He'd had nothing to lose since then. Now that he had Elizabeth to lose, fear twisted in his gut, refusing to ease.

Spencer would find out from him about his life since the accident because he owed it to the man to know the truth about him, about an unspeakable past that embarrassed and mortified him. A past that plagued him and made him unworthy of loving someone like Elizabeth.

If he lay with Elizabeth, his vile hands would soil her and bring her down to his depraved level.

When he'd sent out the invitations to all his friends to come to his country house for a midsummer get-a-away, he'd not thought clearly. Too many of his friends' wives were increasing or had just given birth, leaving the Spencer family the only ones unencumbered to attend.

He was nothing but thrilled Spencer and his family were attending, he'd just hoped Wentworth and Myles would be here to boost his confidence. Not once since his family died, had anyone been to Cliff House. His favorite of his homes by far. His ancestral home was in Northern England, a place he rarely visited. The estate manager was competent and sent him monthly updates.

Indeed, this was the first time he'd entertained, and he prayed it turned out successful with the help of his butler and housekeeper. He had his doubts. Not with the way it had started. Poor Smythe. The runner really needed to find a less dangerous profession. Edward also needed Spencer and Miranda to arrive so he wouldn't be tempted to kiss Elizabeth again...or worse...seduce her.

THE MOMENT AMESBURY closed the door to her bedchamber, Elizabeth ignored the fact that he dismissed her rather abruptly in the library and ran to her bed. Diving facedown she relived the passionate kiss. Rolling onto her back, her quivering fingers touched her lips, she closed her eyes, and sighed deeply. Good Lord, tonight's kiss didn't compare to the short one he'd given her before. He'd used his tongue then, but she'd not participated. Her cheeks heated and she patted them. Innocent debutants gossiped how they thought kissing with tongues unpleasant. Nothing remotely unpleasant about it.

Quite the opposite. It felt right and natural. Somehow she'd known what to do this time once his tongue slipped inside her mouth. Elizabeth suddenly knew how to kiss him back without awkwardness or restraint. Everything in the room had melted away, and nothing existed but the two of them. If strangers kissed, would they feel the same emotions? She hoped and wanted to believe the answer was no. That only Amesbury could make her feel the longing she'd experienced. And she desperately hoped he felt the same only with her.

As she drifted off to sleep curled up on her side, her hands pillowed beneath her cheek, she dreamed of her next kiss with Amesbury and hoped she didn't have to wait an eternity.

CHAPTER FOUR

MARY STARTLED AWAKE SOMETIME DURING THE NIGHT after having bad dreams was disheartened to find Elizabeth had left her alone. Shivering from the cold, as she'd kicked off the coverlet, most likely do to her nightmare. Bits and pieces of her wretched dream came to her. She remembered rivers of blood, people screaming, and Mr. Smythe trying hard to save everyone he could from the monsters attacking a small village. A village, it appeared she and he lived in after they married. Monsters she could hardly see attacked in the dead of night. They were unearthly shadows wielding claymores and guns, killing all they came across—be it woman, man, child, or animal. Smythe and several other men she didn't recognize battled the shadows to no avail. Their weapons went through the transparent beings. Mary saw herself, as though she floated about the carnage, holding an infant and watching wide-eyed out a second story window. The room overflowing with other people trying to hide as well. They believed Smythe could save them. Mary wasn't convinced he could save himself, never mind anyone else.

Blood covered his face, his arms, and stained his white

shirt. He slashed with a sword—long since out of ammunition for his guns and rifle. Not that he would've had time to reload anyway. The monsters didn't reload. Their bullets were one endless stream after another. They could move so fast you never witnessed the actual movement. They went from one spot to another in a blink of an eye.

She took a deep shuddering breath hoping to ease her pounding heart and worried mind. The dream had seemed so real. Still seemed real as she relived it now. Mary's body was exhausted, her mind anguished as though she'd actually lived through it. That it occurred for real, not in a dream. Taking several breaths, in and out, she tried to ignore the images emblazoned on her mind. Because the nightmare didn't end well for any living soul in the village. Not her. Not her baby. Not Smythe.

Mary needed to see him. Needed to convince herself the dream hadn't transpired. That he lived and breathed. After donning her robe over her night rail, she quietly opened her chamber door, not wanting to wake anyone up, not wanting to be found wandering the halls in the middle of the night. Or being found inside Smythe's room at this hour. That would be disastrous.

Taking a moment outside his door to gather herself, she placed one hand over her heart, willing it to calm. When she believed she was composed, she knocked gently, hearing nothing and not expecting to if he were alone and sleeping. She opened the door a crack, peered inside, and let out the breath she'd been holding. A lone candle burned beside the bed, illuminating Mr. Smythe. Dying embers that glowed from the hearth cast shadows throughout the rest of the room and sent an ice-cold chill up her spine. The shadows reminded her of her nightmare.

Opening the door just wide enough for her to sneak inside, she entered and closed it silently. Leaning against the closed, wooden door, she gulped in air feeling as though she'd run across an open field with the hounds of hell chasing her so winded she was. When would her mind stop running away with morbid thoughts and images?

While she caught her breath, her eyes fell on Mr. Smythe lying on his back, looking pale beneath the white covers. Since he spent much time out of doors, his skin was usually darker than most, making him appear much paler now. His contrasting dark brown hair didn't help.

Obviously he'd lost more blood than she'd realized. Silently approaching his bedside on bare feet, she sat on a cold wooden chair someone had pulled next to the bed. She tugged the fabric of her robe up by her neck, pulling it closer together, hoping to ward off the chill. It helped somewhat but not nearly enough to chase the cold away.

"You shouldn't be here."

At hearing his words, her shoulders slumped forward. "Please forgive my intrusion." She stood. "I'll leave you alone then."

"Please stay."

She sat back down, the rejection of seconds ago replaced with joy. "Thank you."

"You shouldn't be here, but I would appreciate it if you would stay." He turned his head to look at her, his brown eyes glazed in pain and something else. "Mr. Spencer would have my hide if he knew you were in here."

"Then it is a good thing he's not arriving for four more days." Since she'd already ignored propriety, she scooted the chair up against the bed and placed her hand on his, shocked at how chilled it felt. "Excuse me a moment." Heading over to the fireplace, Mary placed two large logs on the coals. Using the poker, she poked and prodded until flames licked up thick and bright. Without hesitation she returned to the chair and covered his hand with hers again.

"Thank you."

"For what?"

"The fire. I was lying here pondering how the hell... pardon me...how I was going to drag my broken body over to do what you just did easily enough. For that I'm grateful."

"It was nothing."

His friendly eyes widened and he smiled. "It was everything. People don't usually do for me—I do for them. So please know how grateful I am for your friendship."

She squeezed his hand, removed hers, and curled them together on her lap. "Tell me about your life?"

He made a sound resembling a snort. "There's nothing to tell."

"I beg to differ. I find you fascinating." Oh dear, had she really voiced that out loud? What must he think?

Once again his lips curved into a smile. Mary had no idea how old Mr. Smythe was, perhaps thirty, but when he smiled as he just did, he looked younger.

"You do realize nothing can come of our friendship. It can never go further?"

"Oh dear." Heat suffused her cheeks, scalding them. "Go further?"

His eyes and demeanor turned serious. "What I have to say may shock you. I'm not used to having conversations about feelings with the aristocracy. Indeed, not with a gently bred innocent as yourself, so please accept my apologies if I shock your sensibilities. Where I come from, we speak our mind using plain words. "Ever since we met, the time I was stabbed while working for your brother, and you sat at my bedside, much as you are now, I've had thoughts and dreams of you."

"You have?" Mary was shocked at how breathless her voice sounded.

"Improper thoughts."

"Oh dear." His words had her squirming in the chair. And not just her face heating this time, the warmth encompassed her entire body.

"It would shock you if you knew my thoughts."

"Tell me."

"It's not proper for a lady's ears."

"Tell me anyway." More breathlessness. Heat along with tingles in her body intensified. If only she understood the meaning.

He inhaled a ragged breath and exhaled. "First and foremost I kiss you and hold you in my arms. You're a perfect fit to me. Everything about you is perfect. I worship your body with mine."

She gasped and her whole body engulfed in flames at hearing such improper words.

"Do you understand what that means?"

"Yes. No. Some."

He groaned. "I would give my life to be the man to introduce you to the carnal pleasures of the body. To make love to you." He groaned again and shut his eyes—a pained expression taking over his face. "It is never to be. And for that I'm eternally sorry. You will find a gentleman of worth to marry, and God help him if he doesn't make you happy and treat you respectfully."

Mary could hardly breathe. He sounded so melancholy. "What is your Christian name?"

"Robert. After my father."

"Who is your father?"

"He was a Viscount. My mother was his...mistress."

"Are they both..."

"Dead. Yes."

"I take it he never acknowledged you as his bas..."

"You can say it. Bastard. I am a bastard." He spoke the words with such discussed. "No. According to my mother he loved her and treated her like a princess. When he learned my mother was breeding, he threw her out of the home he'd rented for her with nothing but the clothes on her back and what little coin she'd squirreled away from the years as his mistress. So much for love. Shortly after I was born in the sewers of London the money ran out. You can use your imagination to fill in the rest."

On occasion Mary would glimpse courtesans or mistresses going by in an open carriage. They dressed nicely and looked happy especially if their protector accompanied them. Mary didn't believe their life was a happy one. Always at the whim of their male protector who could decide at any moment to replace them with someone younger and more beautiful. Then there were the street whores who plied their trade on the open streets. Dirty, poor and most likely diseased. Mary's stomach clenched to think of Smythe's mother in such a way.

"I'm too raw to relieve the demoralizing of my mother right now. Or her slow agonizing death from consumption when I was eight. She'd been a gently born daughter of a vicar, fallen in love with my father, given herself to him believing he'd marry her. One cannot marry for a second time when one's wife still lives."

"Robert." Mary leaned forward, grabbing his hand with both of hers. "May I call you Robert?"

"Yes. The viscount, after two years, came looking for my mother. His wife had died in childbirth, the babe as well. He planned to beg my mother for forgiveness. When he realized she whored herself for money, he deserted us again. It was more than my mother could bear. She spiraled into despair. She'd always been choosey when picking a lover, not anymore. A succession of men came and went. Some rich, some poor, some sadistic bastards that beat her. I truly believe she hoped one of them killed her."

"Robert, I don't know what to say." She didn't. She

believed her tears dampening her cheeks said it all. "Can I still be your friend?" The thought of not being his friend pained her heart and the burning lump in her throat made breathing difficult.

"I don't believe your brother would allow it. I think our friendship should end tonight, and I shall go back to being your brother's employee. Nothing more, nothing less. Please forgive me for causing you the anguish I see in your dim blue eyes."

Bemused, Mary pulled her hands back, stood from the chair, and without meeting his eyes, turned and blindly shuffled out of the room. Once in the hallway, she slid to the ground and cried into her hands, hoping nobody heard her. Especially Robert. She didn't want him to feel bad for breaking her heart. It wasn't his fault they lived in different social circles. Not his fault he'd been born a bastard.

WHEN ROBERT HAD RECEIVED a missive from Spencer requesting a Bow Street Runner travel to Hastings to keep his sisters and aunt safe during their travels, he'd temporarily resigned his post as the head of the Bow Street Runners. He didn't trust anyone else when it came to Mary's safekeeping. As soon as he was well enough he would travel back to London and resume his post. It didn't matter what his heart wanted, his mind would have to prevail when it came to Mary. She could never be his and if he prolonged his stay here, it would only make her more miserable. Something he refused to do.

Her sobs reached his ears from beyond the closed door, shattering his already battered body and heart. What he wouldn't give for their circumstances to be different. If she'd been born to a country gentleman, or a vicar, their union would be plausible. However, she was the granddaughter of a countess. Her cousin an earl. So far from his station in life it was laughable. He couldn't bring himself to laugh though. His lungs ached as did the rest of him. As soon as he recovered he would travel back to London. His services wouldn't be needed anymore as Mr. Spencer would be arriving to escort his sisters and aunt back to London. Nor could he picture himself spending a fortnight in the same house as Mary and not approaching to her.

Burying himself in his job had worked for years to dull the pain of his mother's loss. After his mother's death, he'd lived on the streets of St. Giles. He could've taken to thievery, instead he fought against it. What little coin he earned when returning someone's wallet, watch, or reticule or other thing of value, kept him fed and clothed. At the age of ten and five a runner took him under his care. At ten and eight he became a full-fledged runner and head of the respected agency at the age of twenty-five. During those years between ten and five and ten and eight he'd worked hard to lose his gutter speech and speak like a gently bred gentleman. Hence how he blended in well with polite society. If one wanted to work for them, one had to speak and act like them. Which he tried.

His work had helped him recover from his mother's death and his past. It would now have to suffice in easing his burden from loving Mary. Even though he had money and investments, working for members of the *ton* was lucrative, he still lived in a one room boarding house in St. Giles. To be honest, it was one of the very few boarding houses in good repair. Even so Mary would turn and run in horror if she saw his place. Run and not stop until she arrived at Spencer House on Park Street.

He never understood until now why he lived in the sewers of London. Punishment. He punished himself for what happened to his mother. If she never gave birth to him she would still be alive. Still living in a respected section of London. Married to the viscount. For that he punished himself. As long as he lived in the gutters, he would belong in the gutters.

Perhaps if he moved to Cheapside, an upper middle class and respected area of London. He had the means to rent a small house in that area consisting mostly of lawyers, bankers, and businessmen. His heart jumped inside his chest. If he did have a respected address, would Mr. Spencer consider him for Mary? If he showed him his bank accounts and investments proving he could provide for her and any children they had, would he consider Mary for him? Hope soared inside him, and he made a mental list of all the things he needed to accomplish when back in London. For the first time in forever, his future didn't look bleak.

CHAPTER FIVE

AT BREAKFAST THE FOLLOWING DAY IN A BRIGHT YELLOW morning room, Elizabeth found Mary and Amesbury chatting. As she went to pick up a plate on the sideboard, large hands gently brushed hers aside.

"Allow me," Amesbury spoke softly.

"Thank you."

Not wanting to meet his eyes, she stared at the plate as he filled it with coddled eggs, ham, bacon, and a pastry that made her tummy growl. After he placed her plate on the table beside Mary, he waved off the footman and helped her sit himself. He bent low and whispered in her ear, "I'm sorry for last night. I was an idiot."

His warm breath tickled her ear and sent heat cascading down her face, neck, and across her chest. Thankfully she sat next to Mary otherwise her sister would undoubtedly comment on her flushed skin.

"Thank you," she murmured.

After he returned to his seat, picked up his cloth napkin, and dropped it on his lap, he smiled. "I hope your chambers are acceptable to you both and you rested well."

Mary had just taken a sip of her chocolate and almost choked which Elizabeth though odd. "Why yes. I fell asleep almost instantly. The excitement of the day caught up with me. Speaking of yesterday, how is Mr. Smythe?"

"He is remarkably well this morning," Amesbury replied with relief as he cut his ham. I visited him before I came to breakfast. He was actually sitting up, taking broth the cook prepared for him. And I must say I'm thrilled he doesn't want any more laudanum. He hates how it makes him feel. I had the housekeeper throw it away. Vile stuff, laudanum."

"But what if he needs it at night to help him sleep," Mary asked, quite concerned.

"I'm doing as he wishes."

Elizabeth didn't understand Amesbury's objection of laudanum. Indeed, it must have helped him with his pain after he broke his back in the carriage accident. Perhaps that was why. It brought back memories of his own recovery. She prayed Mr. Smythe didn't come down with an infection. They would need the medicine then. She supposed the good doctor could give them more.

"Was the physician in to see him this morning," Mary asked, trying hard to hide her concern but failing, in Elizabeth's eyes anyway.

"Yes. He declared him strong and remarkably healthy, considering the circumstances. Mr. Smythe appeared, although weak from blood loss, ready to get out of bed." He took a bite of ham, chewed and swallowed. "It's Smythe who wants to get out of bed and back to London as soon as possible. The doctor insists he has bed rest for several more days. I wish the doctor good luck."

"Why is he so anxious to return to London?" Elizabeth asked for Mary who had reached for her hand beneath the table when hearing about his return to London. "I thought he planned to spend the fortnight here and ride back with us?"

"Perhaps something has come up and he's needed back in London."

"Did he receive a missive?" Mary asked, her voice cracking with emotion.

Amesbury frowned. "Not that I'm aware. Perhaps he feels he let your brother down and prefers to leave before he and Miranda arrive."

"Yes," Elizabeth chimed in, "that must be it. Although Spencer would think him a hero for saving us."

Just then Violet entered the morning room, looking lovely, but tired, in a seafoam green muslin day dress and matching turban. "That is right. He is a hero. More than once to me. I would be dead if not for him."

"Oh Auntie Violet," Elizabeth said, "yesterday's events must have brought back your abduction. How are you faring?"

She patted her turban. "Better than I thought, all things considered. I'm just very thankful neither of you girls were hurt. You have so many years ahead of you." When Violet turned her back and busied herself filling her plate, the subject closed. Elizabeth didn't want to keep bringing up the events with her now dead third husband, Mr. Henry Baker. Or yesterday's events if Violet didn't want to discuss them.

As to Mr. Smythe wanting to leave, it would break Mary's heart. Spencer would never be disappointed with him. He did what he'd been hired to do. He took bullets for them. Could've died for them. Pray, thank God, he didn't. Mary dropped her napkin beside her unfinished plate and stood abruptly.

"I do believe I feel a headache coming on. I'm going to retire to my room." Mary's voice waivered as though she fought back tears.

"Mary seems upset," Amesbury said over the delicate china cup he held, no doubt holding strong coffee. Elizabeth didn't know how anyone could drink the vile tasting stuff. It was all the rage in England though. She'd stick to her tea and chocolate. "Is there something I don't know about?" he added.

She did not want to share Mary's confidences with Amesbury. How he would react, she didn't have any indication. As much as she believed she knew him, there was so much more to the man than she ever thought possible. And she had a feeling he hid so much more. "My sister does suffer from migraines. Yesterday's events probably kept her up last night no matter if she said she slept well."

"I hope the poor dear feels better," Violet said as a footman helped her take her seat in Mary's vacated one. "I used to suffer from migraines. Didn't leave my bed for days at a time. Thank goodness I outgrew them."

"Oh, Miss Violet," Amesbury said with a mischievous grin, "how can you have outgrown something. You are still in your prime."

"I thank you Lord Amesbury." She smiled. "I'm not much older than you, but sadly our society thinks differently about men and women's ages. You are still in your prime while I have one foot in the grave. It's highly ridiculous. I'm not so old I wouldn't mind snaring myself a forth husband." She laughed, breaking the awkwardness of her last sentence.

It made Elizabeth and Amesbury lock amused eyes. Had Violet been sincere in wanting a forth husband? Hadn't she been through enough burying the first two sadly, then gladly the third, who found himself buried in a pauper's grave. Even that was too good for the man. She also knew Violet was forty years old. She believed Amesbury to be five and thirty. Violet still had her youthful figure as she'd never given birth. Not that she knew of. Her thick dark hair had some gray streaked through it. Her face was still beautiful with very few age lines. Elizabeth hoped there was an older gentleman who would appreciate her loveliness.

Not any time soon though. People no doubt still gossiped about her and Miranda's ordeal with that rat of a husband and abductor. Perhaps when next Season came around.

"Have you anything planned for this day, Amesbury? The sun is shining and no doubt it's warm outside," Elizabeth asked, hoping for a little time out of doors to boost her mood.

"I thought perhaps we could take a ride and I could show you, Mary, and Violet the estate's extensive property."

"Not me, dear Amesbury, I don't ride," Violet said apologetically.

"Well perhaps you and Mary could accompany me?"

"I don't believe Mary will be up to riding with her feeling under the weather," Violet said.

"Will you allow Elizabeth to ride with me?"

"That will be acceptable. That is if she wishes too?"

Elizabeth answered trying to ignore the excitement humming inside her. "Why I would love to see the grounds of Cliff House. It is so much quieter here than at Bridgeton Manor in Dover. Lately it's become such a hustle and bustle port with inns and drinking establishments popping up everywhere in town. My cousin's house is situated on many aches, we aren't near the town, but still. We used to be allowed to ride to town with just our maid for companionship, but not anymore. Too many unsavory people lurking about."

"You won't find that here. My estate is quite isolated although Hastings is becoming more and more populated. I'm glad the house is situated far back from the coast you can't even see the water from here. When my father purchased this place when I was around five, I recall he and my mother joking about why in the world the place was called

Cliff House when it didn't overlook the cliffs. I can't recall what they said, but they never changed the name, nor will I.

"It is a lovely name. Before we leave, I will see how Mary is fairing." She looked at the clock on the wall. "Will half ten be fine."

Amesbury nodded. "Perfect. I will meet you out front with our mounts."

MARY SELDOM GOT ANGRY. Most everyday occurrences were not worth it. But this? This man thinking he would leave before he healed, and most likely without so much as a by your leave, irked her anger. Headache. She hadn't lied about the pain in her head, it came upon her so suddenly when she found out about Robert.

Oh, she knew what he said to her last evening. That there would, could never be, anything between them. However, she disagreed. Her family wasn't so high and mighty they didn't take into account someone's self-worth as a person over title and money. Besides, if it came down to money, she had a dowry. No idea how much, but her family was wealthy so it must be plentiful. And honestly, if she did marry Robert, her family would never disown her, leaving her destitute. Her grandmother would never allow it. She loved her too much. By now she stood outside his room hoping to take control of her anger. Most men didn't take kindly to being berated by a woman. She imagined Robert was no different.

Stopping to take several soothing breaths, she wrapped her knuckles lightly against his door and held her breath while she waited.

"Come in."

Before she opened the door she closed her eyes, trying to calm her racing heart. She knew it would be disastrous if she was found in a bachelor's room, but she'd tempted fate already and besides what was the worst that could happen? Spencer would force Robert to marry her. She would sing out with joy! Then something else she'd never thought of plagued her mind. Spencer could make her marry someone else. Someone in their social circle. It didn't actually have to be Robert. It had been known to happen. A young lady of the *ton* found with someone not quite up to snuff, so her family paid someone socially acceptable to marry her instead. She shuttered, how awful.

If Mary wanted to save her heart from excruciating pain, she had to be honest with Robert about her feelings. She could no longer think of him as Mr. Smythe. To her he was Robert. Hopefully *her* Robert.

The idea of expressing her feelings to him, actually saying the words love, frightened her to the core. Would he laugh at her? Ridicule her for falling in love with a commoner. Actually worse than a commoner—a bastard? She shivered. To her it didn't matter what his lineage was. Nothing would ever change her feelings for him.

Finally experiencing a hint of bravery, she opened the door and quietly slipped inside only to be frozen to the floor when her eyes locked with Robert's intense ones as he stood fully dressed beside his bed with his arm in a sling. She shivered and hugged her waist.

"Are you cold, Miss Spencer?"

He looked and sounded stronger than he had last evening. Although she couldn't believe he would leave until another day or two passed—hopefully heeding the physician's instructions. "No."

"He tilted his head."

"Well, perhaps a bit. Would you like me to stoke the fire?"

"No. I'm hot as hades." He blanched. "Pardon."

As her feet ate up the distance between them, she said,

"You do not have to watch your language with me. My brother doesn't while in the privacy of our home, to my grandmother and mother's dismay. Or more my grandmother, my mother hardly ever concerns herself with the affairs of her children."

"I'm sorry."

Mary blushed hot, which eased her chilled body. "No. I'm sorry. After what you told me about your mother, I should not complain as mine still lives."

"Don't be. I came to terms with the circumstances of my birth and the death of my mother many years ago. Nothing comes from obsessing about one's past. It doesn't change facts."

Mary didn't believe him. Indeed, he may have come to terms with his lot in life, but the melancholy expression on his face admitted he still wished his mother lived and his life had been different.

"Lord Amesbury told me the physician visited you this morning."

"Yes. He thinks I need to stay in this bed for several more days." He shrugged his good shoulder. "He doesn't know anything about me. I'll be ready to ride back to London tomorrow. The bleeding has stopped and no infection has set in."

She tried to hide her disappointment at his desire to leave so soon after arriving. "Robert." She moved closer to his side, and against etiquette's rules, took his free hand in hers. The skin to skin contact startled her. "Why are you in such a hurry to leave? I thought you were staying for a fortnight to escort us back to London."

"Your brother can take my place. My services are no longer required, but they are needed back in London."

"Robert..." She pulled her hands away and knotted them together in front of her. Closing her eyes for courage she whispered, "Robert...I...I wish you would stay." Her slippers became the focus of her attention. Because if she looked at Robert, she might embarrass herself and cry. "I have feelings for you. Strong feelings. Perhaps even love." She exhaled and fought a sense of vertigo as the room spun around her.

"Miss Spencer..."

"Please call me Mary."

"Very well, Mary. We have been over this before. Last night in fact. To save both of us heartache and pain for what will never be, please for the love of God, leave me be." He made a sound like a tortured animal. "I can't do this. My feelings for you grow more each day. I don't know if I can control them or myself if you keep insinuating yourself in my presence."

"Oh." She tried not to take offense from his words which were a flurry of contradictions.

"Please accept my apologies. I've hurt your feelings. I can see it on your face and in your eyes."

Her fingers went to stop her tears from leaking out of her eyes. "I'll leave you to your solitude. I'll not bother you again. I'm terribly sorry to have forced my person on you." As she pivoted around a hand shot out and curled around her upper arm.

"Please don't. I'm being an arse." Robert's words and expression both apologetic and desperate.

Before Mary could move or think, he pulled her against him with his good arm, wincing for a moment before lowering his face to hers and kissing her softly. Robert's lips were warm, soft, and pliant. As this was her first kiss, she didn't know what to expect. But the softness and gentleness of his lips was not it. The sound of a moan traveled to her ears, whether it came from Robert or her, she didn't know. Perhaps both of them.

His large hand splayed against the small of her back,

pulling her even closer to his body. A hard bulge nudged against her lower stomach, and this time it was Robert who moaned. His lips coaxed hers apart, and she tried not to act shocked when his tongue entered her mouth and swirled around and around until she joined her tongue with his and they twirled and danced together.

"Mary," Robert breathed against her lips. "You need to tell me to stop because I can't."

"Can't stop what," she murmured into his mouth. Her head tingled and her body felt weightless, as though she were floating in his arms.

"My dear innocent Mary." He went to step back and she reached out pulling him close again.

"No. This is what I want. You are what I want." Even though she didn't understand the depth of her words or what her body craved, she couldn't let him go. "Please kiss me again."

And he did. His hand cupped her cheek reverently as he dropped his head and kissed her again. Not the same as before. This kiss, even with her inexperience, conveyed something altogether different than the gentle one of before. His mouth devoured hers. He used his tongue, his teeth as he plundered her mouth, making her grip one side of his waist-coat lapel to steady herself as her knees buckled. Time stood still around them. His upper body shifted slightly, and his questing hand cupped her breast. His fingers circled her nipple until it hardened, and to her surprise he pinched her, and she felt the sensation down low between her thighs. Her womanhood awakened, and she needed him to do something to satisfy it.

The room and all its contents melted into nothingness. The only sound was a buzzing in her ears. His hand skimmed down her side, across her stomach and found her woman-hood. The tips of his fingers touched her there through the fabric of her skirts and she gasped with shock. Shock that turned to pleasure as he continued seeking her core. Her hips seemed to know what to do as they pushed against his hand, seeking something elusive and mysterious.

Every muscle in her body liquefied. Moist heat, like she'd never experienced before, pooled between her legs. Her lower stomach coiled up tight. Something unlike anything she ever experienced crashed into her and she broke the kiss, buried her face against Robert's chest, and gasped loudly trying to catch her breath.

It seemed forever before she trusted herself to speak. "What happened?" she whispered as her body continued to tremble.

The sound of Robert chuckling was music to her ears. "You, my dear, sensual innocent, experienced your first sexual release."

She gasped, raised her head and looked into Robert's beautiful molten brown eyes.

"How's that possible? It didn't hurt. Can I become with child?" As she said the words, panic hit her and she trembled.

He held her close to his heart. "No sweetheart. Much more needs to occur for that to happen. I give you my word, I will never compromise you in that way. Just for your knowledge, there are many ways to pleasure a woman without risking breeding or taking her virginity."

"What about you, are there ways to pleasure a man without..." She couldn't bring herself to look at him as her cheeks were aflame with embarrassment.

"Yes," he choked out.

"Will you show me?"

Something resembling both a groan and laugh came from Robert. "My dear, Mary, you will be the death of me."

"Mary," Elizabeth called to her from behind the closed

door. "I know you are in there. Please come out now. I must speak to you."

"I must go." Mary hurried from the room, not glancing back at Robert. Afraid to look because if she did she would blush even deeper. One look at her face and Elizabeth would know something had happened.

AFTER MARY LEFT, Robert could still see her pink cheeks, her soft blue eyes, and her pert little nose causing his heart to split wide open. He should have forced her to leave the moment she entered his room. Said hurtful words, anything to not feel the heartache that would surely come to both of them. He couldn't do it. He would do anything within his power to never hurt her. Never be the cause of her tears as he'd witnessed only minutes ago. He'd never realized until then how much her tears would affect him. Women had cried in his presence before, even women he'd bedded, but never had he felt anything. Well, perhaps remorse or guilt, but not feelings related to the heart.

Mary? What was he to do about Mary and his all-encompassing feelings for her? Kissing her had singlehandedly been the most precious, intimate, and loving experience of his entire eight and twenty years of life. There were no words to describe the shock that rocked his body when she'd exploded in his arms, causing him to nearly come in his breeches. How embarrassing that would have been. Mary was a true innocent, although not so much anymore, she would not have understood the wet stain on his buff breeches. God forbid she thought he'd pissed himself.

The entire time Robert held Mary in his arms, kissing and fondling her, his upper body burned like fire. Not just from his wounds but from the ache inside his chest knowing this may possibly be the one and only time he held her so dear to his heart. He was a realist and didn't for the life of him expect Mr. Spencer to allow him to court his sister. The hell with courting, he wanted to marry her and spend the rest of his life showering her with his love. To appease her, he would stay, at least until her brother arrived and he could confront him with his attentions. He owed it to Mary to do so. Because he didn't want either of them to wonder for the rest of their lives if they could've been together.

However, he could see it now. Spencer would have Amesbury's burliest male servant throw his sorry arse out, and then beat him to within an inch of his life. His body vibrated from head to toe. It was no less than he deserved for trying to be better than he was.

He'd taken advantage of a member of the aristocracy. He could see Newgate in his future clear as day. He wouldn't last twenty-four hours before being killed as he'd sent too many criminals to that horrific place. One of them would kill him in his sleep while the guards changed shifts. Happened all the time. The thought of Mary mourning over him was like a stab to his heart. He wished Spencer would arrive so he could get this over with.

CHAPTER SIX

THE MOMENT MARY EXITED SMYTHE'S CHAMBER, Elizabeth knew by her disheveled hair and clothes and the strawberry red of her cheeks that something had happened. "Come." She took her sister's hand, pulling her down the hall and another until they were in the privacy of her bedchamber. Both taking a seat on the chaise facing the warm hearth, Elizabeth turned and said, "Tell me. I'm dying to know what happened."

To her horror Mary buried her face in her hands and cried. Elizabeth placed her hand on her back and rubbed in circles. "There, there, it can't be all that bad."

Mary sniffled and cleared her throat. "I'm not crying because I'm sad. It's because I'm overwhelmed with feelings. Feelings I don't quite understand and then there is the love bursting from my heart for Robert."

"It's Robert now, is it?"

Mary giggled, raised her head, and wiped her tears away. "Yes. Such a strong name. Robert Smythe."

"I can't believe you are calling each other by your first names, and I'm still referring to Amesbury as...well...Amesbury. He has yet to ask me to call him Edward. Perhaps I shall request him to call me Elizabeth and without insulting me he must insist I call him Edward."

"Yes, indeed, that will work."

"Is it my imagination or does Edward, I can call him Edward to you, seem distant and moody since we arrived. I truly thought he invited us here specifically so he could get to know me better. What a stupid fool I am. I know he had many guests on his list, and most couldn't come, and our brother and Miranda will be here in a few days, but still, he seems distant. Every other time we attended gatherings at country estates, there is always much planned and many things to do. If it is at an estate of a single gentleman, usually they have a female relative to act as hostess." She paused then gasped. "He has no relatives, female or male. Perhaps I should offer my services to act as his..."

"No," Mary interjected. "That would be too presumptuous. Besides, it was only going to be close friends attending. I think it was meant to be relaxing and an intimate affair. I don't believe Amesbury meant to have all those silly games, planned rides, and hunts like most country gatherings."

"Oh my God." Elizabeth jumped up. I forgot Edward asked me to go riding. It must be past time I'm supposed to meet him downstairs." She went to the wardrobe and grabbed her burgundy riding habit and matching hat. "Please help me change. I hope he doesn't think I'm not joining him."

Elizabeth practically ran through the halls and down the stairs and out the door so fast the doorman never had a chance to open the door for her. She turned the knob and swung it open in a flash, then paused to catch her breath and smooth her skirts. She also took a moment to watch Amesbury as his back faced her.

Calm now, she said, "Forgive me for being tardy."

At the sound of her voice, he pivoted and smiled, taking

the air from her lungs. Amesbury had always been beyond handsome. Standing now in his buff riding breeches that hugged his thighs, his cut-away dark brown riding coat, cream waistcoat and cream linen shirt and cravat left her speechless. And that was before she took in his face, his thick brown wavy hair, hazel eyes, not green or blue, but something in-between. His jaw was finely chiseled and his nose slightly crooked. She recalled he'd broken it once in a fight at Eaton. Wentworth, Myles, and Amesbury, she'd heard were hellions back in their Eaton days. Truth be told, they were known as the rakehells until several years ago. Her heart flipped.

"All is forgiven. Come, meet your horse." Something had changed between breakfast and now. Amesbury appeared relaxed as he moved with liquid grace to stand beside her mount. "Her name is Peppermint. She is calm, graceful, and not easily spooked." He laughed. "She also likes peppermint candies. I keep a supply in my pocket for her." As he spoke the horse nudged his side, no doubt smelling the treat.

A groomsman came forward with a wooden block, but Amesbury waved him off and he helped her mount Peppermint himself. Yes, indeed, something had changed. This was the Amesbury she'd known and fallen in love with in London during the beginning of the Season. What had made him moody and distant since she arrived she couldn't say. Of course, it could have something to do with them being attacked by highwaymen and Mr. Smythe being shot. Once she was settled in the sidesaddle, his hands lingered on her waist, their eyes met, and she found herself drowning in the deep depths of his radiant orbs.

He bowed his head ever so slightly, turned, and mounted his horse a tad awkwardly which surprised her. "I had cook pack us a picnic lunch." Until now she hadn't noticed the saddlebags. "It's sure to be a treat."

Amesbury clicked his reins and set his horse's pace at a

slow walk. She and Amesbury rode side by side in silence for a time until he spoke. "I thought we could first explore the village and then part of my lands. There is a meadow of wild-flowers still blooming, although they are starting to wilt with the cooling nights. Or we could ride toward the cliffs and the channel."

"I see cliffs and the English Channel in Dover quite often, I would love to see the village and the meadow. How many acres do you have?"

"As this is not my ancestral home, the lands are not as great in size, nor do I have as many tenants. I have a little over a thousand acres and thirty tenants." Turning his head, their eyes met and her heart leaped at the longing she glimpsed. She'd never really thought about Edward being lonely because he had a closeness with Wentworth and Myles, not to mention, a friendship with Bridgeton and Spencer. However, now that she thought about it, when he retired to his home at night, he was alone. Had been alone since his family died. What did he do to occupy his time? Her heart constricted. She didn't think she could be alone. She and Mary were as close as sisters could be, making Elizabeth wonder how she would live without Mary when one of them married.

With her woolgathering, she found herself far behind Edward. She clicked the reins and sent Peppermint into a trot and found herself next to Edward in no time.

"I was wondering when you'd realize you were lagging behind," Amesbury said with a chuckle.

"My mind wandered. I apologize."

"None necessary, and please call me Edward."

Elizabeth wanted to dismount and twirl around in joy. Finally, Edward gave her permission to use his Christian name. "Then you must call me Elizabeth."

They rode to the village, bustling with fishmongers, farmers, and flower peddlers hocking their wares. Edward and she visited shops and he introduced her to the shopkeepers. He purchased lavender and vanilla scented soap for her at the soap store and a posy of heather and daisies from the flower vender even though she could pick her own in the meadow. How thoughtful of Edward. Then they rode aimlessly around for almost an hour.

With the village far behind, Elizabeth, feeling elated after Edward's thoughtfulness to her, kicked her horse into a canter and took off over the field of tall green grasses. Eventually her horse slowed and Edward came up beside her.

"I thought you would race me." She said catching her breath.

He grinned at her and her heart melted. "I enjoyed the view from behind."

Realizing what Edward would have been watching, had Elizabeth's cheeks heating with embarrassment.

"Here we are." Edward dismounted then helped her as they stood in the middle of wildflowers as far as the eye could see. She did admit the colors were not as vibrant as they would have been in the early days of summer, but they still took her breath away. She inhaled deeply, reveling in the aroma of lavender as it overpowered all other scents.

Edward tied their horses to an ancient, gnarly tree with most of its bark gone. He opened his saddlebag and spread a blanket on the ground beneath another old tree, trying not to squish the flowers. How considerate of him. How many gentlemen would worry about the wildflowers.

"Please sit. I'll bring the food over."

Elizabeth, careful of her skirts, sat down on one side of the blanket, crossed her legs beneath her skirts, making sure they were covered. Her eyes drifted to Edward as he juggled several items, a bottle of wine and two glasses in his large capable hands, making her wonder what those hands would feel like on her body. Heat suffused her cheeks and she turned away lest he see her blush. There were times, many times, she wished mothers would share with their daughters the intimacies of the marriage bed when they came out for their first Season instead of waiting until the night before they said their marriage vows. Of course, in her case, it would be her grandmother, how mortifying. Oh, Elizabeth had knowledge that came from books, but somehow pictures only made her imagination worse. When Miranda arrived, she planned on waylaying her into telling her and Mary everything involved in making love with a man.

"You seem to be woolgathering again, Elizabeth. Am I that boring?"

Startled, her cheeks warming once again, she replied, "Not at all. I was looking around and thinking how lovely your place is," she lied. She had to. She couldn't very well tell him her wayward thoughts.

"I am fortunate. Too bad I don't spend much time here." He opened the wine, poured her a glass, and handed it to her, then poured his. "I prefer the hustle and bustle of London. Even in the dead of winter or in the heat of summer when most of the *ton* is at their country estates. There is still some gathering or another to attend and my clubs never close." He drank deeply of his glass while Elizabeth sipped the sweet wine. How did he know she liked her wine on the sweet side?

"I never thought much about what others were doing when we retire to the country. Would you like me to serve lunch?"

"No." His lips twisted up into a crooked grin, taking her breath away. "You are my guest." He filled two plates with finger sandwiches, bits of chicken, fruit and cheese. He handed over her plate with a napkin and smiled. "*Bon appétit.* Cook informed me she made raspberry tart for dessert."

"Oh yummy, my favorite," Elizabeth said between bites of her cucumber sandwich. "How did she know?"

Edward shrugged his shoulders and looked as though he had a secret. "No idea. Lucky guess I think." He popped a grape in his mouth and took his time chewing all the while never taking his eyes off her. "Cook made the raspberry tart because it's my favorite."

Smiling with excitement, Elizabeth said, "We've something in common then."

Placing his now empty plate beside him on the blanket, he leaned toward her. "I think we have more in common than that." He reached out, her eyes riveted on his hand, and he cupped her cheek. The contact took her breath away. "I hope, no...think, we have other things in common than tarts."

The intensity of his eyes and the warmth of his hand had her leaning toward him, anticipating his lips connecting with hers. Instead they stayed, swaying toward each other, eyes locked in an emotional discovery. She uncurled her legs so they were straight out, ignoring the sudden air wafting up her skirts. Time evaporated, the wildflowers disappeared around them, it felt as though they were floating on a cloud, the only two people in the world. Only now mattered. Time and consequences weren't relevant.

Edward blinked, breaking the spell. He pulled back, and she almost fell to the blanket in a frustrated huff. Instead she busied her hands covering her ankles with her skirts and focusing straight ahead. Her heart thumped wildly inside her chest, and she inhaled deeply several times. It felt as though she'd been holding her breath for hours.

"You do love to get lost in your thoughts." He held out a small plate filled with tart.

Heat infused her cheeks again. She didn't think she'd ever blushed this much before. "Thank you. This looks delicious."

"I assure you, it is."

They sat in silence as each ate their dessert. She had to admit it was the best raspberry tart she'd ever tasted. Perhaps his cook wouldn't mind sharing her recipe with her brother's cook. Of course, how did one accomplish that without insulting her brother's cook? Perhaps that wasn't the best idea.

She barely noticed when Edward took her empty plate from her hand. Her eyes did widen when he lay down on his back, his arms behind his head making a pillow. "Why don't you relax. The sun is warm and we have no place to be but here." He sat back up, removed his riding jacket, folded it and placed it on the blanket beside him. "Here. A pillow to cushion your head."

Unable to ignore the sleepiness the food gave her, she curled on her side facing him, careful to adjust her skirts so she was covered. She didn't want him to think her forward even if she wanted him to remove her clothing. Even she shocked herself with her thoughts at times.

His scent of sandalwood and masculinity wafted up from her pillow consisting of his riding jacket. The scent infused her and she tingled all over. It took great self-control not to bury her face in his jacket and inhale deeply.

"Comfortable?"

"Hmmm, very."

"I'm going to close my eyes for a spell. You might want to do the same?"

"Hmmm, I already am." It didn't take more than a minute for Elizabeth to realize how tired she was.

WHEN EDWARD NOTICED Elizabeth's breathing become steady and even, he turned onto his side, ignoring the pain in his back and legs, and watched her in slumber. She'd had telltale signs of appearing sleepy, so he thought a nap in the outdoor sunshine would do her good, which was why he'd pretended to be sleepy as well. When in fact all he wanted to do was watch over her while she slumbered. His chest ached with a protectiveness he'd never felt before. Not even with his sister. Well, not true, he felt very protective of Jane when she lived, but with Elizabeth it went beyond that. The desire and need to safeguard her with his body, heart, and soul took over his every thought when with her.

And yet a part of him felt terrified of the depths of his feelings for her. Everyone he ever loved died. Was his love cursed? Would his love for Elizabeth be her ultimate demise? Lunch churned inside his stomach. He swallowed and fought the nausea.

A wayward chestnut brown curl had fallen across her forward and onto her milky white eyelid. Gently he brushed it aside, and while he did, he couldn't help but rub the silky strands between his fingers. A little purr escaped her lips, and he pulled his hand back quickly, not wanting to wake her yet. In time he would. In slumber she resembled a fairy princess. Her features relaxed and perfectly formed, kicked him in the gut with need. Was she a princess who needed rescuing? No. Elizabeth had a wonderful family who treated her with love and care.

If she needed rescuing it would make his life easier. Because he felt less than worthy of her. She had a perfect life. Marrying her, in his mind, would not be fair to her. Not with his skeletons. If she were a young lady with a wicked step-mother, marrying her would be the kind thing.

Hell, he wanted to marry Elizabeth more than anything else in this blasted world. He had a problem though. How to forgive himself for all his past sins, so in truth, he could prove worthy of her. Forgiving himself was his downfall. How did one love someone else, truly give one's heart to them, when one hated oneself? At times like this, he wished Wentworth and Myles were close by. The two of them spoke very candidly, they wouldn't let him shirk his feelings. Feelings? Since when did gentlemen talk about feelings? Perhaps most didn't, but the three of them did. It was how they had survived the devastating things slung at them. Although to be truthful with himself, nothing they did was self-inflicted as some of his demons were.

Enough self-pity. It was high time he lived for today and gave his heart to the lady sleeping beside him.

Gently, he brushed his index finger ever so lightly down her cheek, down her neck, pausing to feel the blood pumping through her veins. Emotions crashed inside him, making his hand tremble along with his heart. His finger continued along down her neck and traced her delicate collarbone. He knew the instant she awoke. Her breathing changed, causing the rise and fall of her chest to increase. Her luscious pink lips curled up into a sleepy smile, and her dreamy blue eyes fluttered open ever so slowly, causing him to groan with need. Never had he seen such an erotic sight as Elizabeth glancing at him with innocent eyes glazed with desire.

"Edward?"

"Elizabeth?"

He rolled on top of her, one of his legs nestled in the juncture of her thighs. He kissed her mouth gently several times before moving down her neck, across her chest, and up the other side. Her body shivered and her hips rose against his leg. With a sigh he took her lips again. Not so gently this time, it only took a second for Elizabeth to open her mouth to him, allowing his tongue to thrust inside and explore. Her arms wrapped around his neck, holding him in place while her fingers tangled in his hair. Each and every time he intensified the kiss, she tugged his hair. The shock of the pain and the relief that came as she eased her fingers sent an inferno of desire to smolder inside his veins. He wanted her like he'd never wanted anyone or anything before. *Make her yours* screamed inside his head.

Breaking their kiss, he dragged in air as he concentrated on her lovely face. "If we don't stop, you do realize what will happen?"

A becoming blush spread from her face down her chest and up to her ears, making her look even more beautiful if possible. "Yes to most," she whispered, and his eyes were drawn to her swollen lips.

"Is this what you want? Because if we join our bodies here and now, we join our hearts, souls, and lives for eternity?"

Her fingers, still entangled in his hair, tightened at the same time she murmured, "Yes...yes...to it all. I want it all with you, Edward."

Her answer was all he needed to hear, and Edward sighed deeply with relief. Finally, Elizabeth would be his whether he truly deserved her or not.

HAD ELIZABETH REALLY SAID YES? The joining of their bodies, for the first time, was going to happen outside surrounded by wildflowers, birds, and other daytime creatures. Elizabeth's heart accelerated to near bursting from her chest. There was no more beautiful place to give herself to Edward than here. She'd said yes, so why was he still looking at her with wonder in his eyes when he should be doing...something.

The more he stared into her face with awe, the more nervous and self-conscious she became. So to speed things along and hide her insecurity, she tugged his head down to hers and kissed him. Her tongue delved inside his mouth and she tasted him. Wine and raspberries tingled against her tongue, and she moaned from the pleasurable taste.

While they kissed, Edward's hands make fast work of the frog closures on her riding jacket and the laces on her blouse. He tugged down the front of her bodice, and cool air breezed across her exposed breasts sending her body aquiver. His lips moved from her mouth, placing feather light kisses down her neck and across her chest. He swirled his tongue around one nipple then the other and caused sensations to furl inside her belly and a warm heat to melt in the apex of her thighs.

"Hmmm," she moaned as he suckled one nipple, and one hand shimmied up the inside of her skirts and untied the waist of her pantaloons. Her hips lifted, allowing him to slip them down around her ankles.

His head rose and he chuckled. "I forgot about your riding boots."

"Me too."

Edward removed her boots, spending time inspecting her exposed skin, causing gooseflesh to break out on her legs. One large hand skimmed up her thighs, bunching her skirts up around her waist and all the while he kissed her. The cool breeze hitting her core caused her to shiver. She would die of mortification if Edward could see her exposed womanhood, but he couldn't. Then Elizabeth gasped and arched her back when his hand cupped her there. His fingers played with her curls, then parted her folds and found the center of her, and she tried to swallow her moans.

He chuckled against her mouth. "No one can hear you except me. And let me explain something, when you make those pleasurable sounds in the back of your throat my body burns for you." He ground his hips against her, and she felt the hard length of him through his riding breeches. "Feel me. That is for you. Only you, for the rest of time, my love."

Elizabeth had seen pictures of naked statues and pictures

of men in books, but she had no idea how that hard thing in his pants would go inside her. She went to voice her concerns when he moved down her body, pushed her skirts higher, spread her legs and buried his face there. "Edward? Surely you are not? Oh dear...hmmm."

"Relax and enjoy my love."

She sighed, rested her head back on his riding jacket pillow and let her body feel. Shock and embarrassment quickly turned over to pleasure, and all her inhibitions vanished. Edward's tongue swirled around her and sucked on her nub while he slid a finger inside her, making her hips thrust off the ground trying to get closer to his mouth and hand. If he could see her now, her face would be as red as strawberries. Lust and need took over as her body craved something beyond her knowledge and reach. Until...it happened. And when it did, her life altered, the earth shattered, and the sun exploded, sending beams of warm light to surround her and curl about her body and heart.

Elizabeth couldn't move, her body spent and intent to lie beneath Edward and bask in the warm glow surrounding them both. But Edward had other ideas. He moved up her body, his hand still playing down between her thighs, and he placed light kisses everywhere while making sounds of pleasure. His hand left her center, and she heard and felt him undoing the front placket of his riding breeches until she felt something warm, hard, and silky against her thigh.

"I love you," Edward said against her ear. "I wanted you to know before we..."

Her body still languid, her heart burst alive with his words. "I love you as well. Have since I first met you." Her hands wrapped around his neck. "Make me yours. Make love to me."

Edward groaned as he nudged his manhood at the juncture of her thighs. "Try to stay relaxed. I'll make this as pain-less as possible."

"How much will it hurt," she whispered as her body tensed.

"Never been with a virgin. But from everything I've read, it only hurts briefly, and only the first time." While he spoke his fingers were playing between her thighs again, and she felt the feelings she now knew were sexual need curl inside her belly as heat infused her womanhood.

"Now Edward, I'm ready."

"Elizabeth..." He nudged again at her opening and she arched up against him. His member slid in a little at a time. He took her mouth in a searing kiss and pushed all the way inside past her barrier. Her body tensed from the invasion and pain. Edward didn't move. His lips separated from hers, his breath heavy against her mouth. "I'm sorry. Did it hurt much?"

"For a minute."

"Does it hurt now?"

"Mildly."

"Can I finish and take you with me?"

Finish? What did he mean by finish? "What does that mean?"

He grinned. "Would you like to find out?"

The pain between her thighs eased as she relaxed, knowing she was with Edward and he loved her and would never intentionally hurt her. "Yes," she whispered.

Before she'd finished saying yes, Edward crashed his mouth to hers and kissed her greedily. His hips thrust forward and released, causing his member to move within her body, licking her flames of arousal. Her legs wrapped around his waist, and she thrust her hips, trying to find a rhythm with him. Push, pull, up, down, it didn't matter as long as they were joined with the same goal in mind.

Just as before her body trembled all over, and this time she didn't hold her moans in, she screamed as Edward thrust one last time before his body tightened, warm moisture flooded her insides, and he collapsed on top of her.

Not long after they dressed the air chilled as the sun lowered on the horizon. Edward had a hard time keeping his hands off her as he assisted her with her clothes. Once Elizabeth was presentable, or as presentable as one could be without a looking glass to inspect her hair and clothing, she helped Edward with his shirt. She would ignore her disappointment that he'd already donned his breeches, hiding that part of him that fascinated her. She'd never had a chance to get a good look at it or touch it. Next time she vowed to explore his body as he'd done hers.

As they rode back to Cliff House, words were few, but stolen looks, smiles, and glances going back and forth between them were numerous, thrilling her. After what they'd shared, something Elizabeth knew would forever be etched in her heart and mind as the best day of her life, words were not needed. Expressions and emotions didn't lie. At least she didn't think they did. At least not in this case.

As they approached the front steps of the manor, a groom waited to take the horses and Elizabeth saw her brother's coach parked front and center. The excitement at her brother arriving days early quickly turned to dread. Spencer and Miranda couldn't see her in this disheveled condition. They would know at once what transpired between her and Edward. It didn't matter that Edward proposed, he had, hadn't he? Spencer would be furious. With any luck, they would be either in the drawing room or their assigned chambers, and she could ascend the stairs fast and quietly. In no time at all she would be in the safety of her room, and with the help of the ladies' maid her and Mary shared, made presentable again before she welcomed the rest of her family.

Edward touched her arm and she settled. "I would presume they are waiting in the drawing room for us. I will go and keep them occupied while you retire to your room and prepare yourself." He leaned close to her ear. "Please be quick, so Spencer doesn't get suspicious."

CHAPTER SEVEN

After Amesbury and Elizabeth left for their ride, Mary changed her clothing into her prettiest and favorite day dress. A blue muslin that complimented her blonde hair and blue eyes. She even had the ladies' maid Amesbury provided her, redo her hair into a whimsical style. The whole time her pulse soared, and she tried to hide her excitement at what she planned to do. After she dismissed the maid, she entered the hallway and made her way down another hall and another until she stood outside Mr. Smythe's room. Robert. He told her to call him Robert. Before anyone saw her, she knocked, and without waiting for a reply, slipped inside the room. Once inside, she noticed several things. The curtains were open, letting in light, a fire blazed in the hearth and Robert sat facing it. His face, however, was turned toward her and his eyes alight with curiosity.

"Robert," she whispered as she moved to his side. "How are you feeling?"

"Almost like new. I hardly hurt at all. Am I mistaken but didn't you already visit me this morn?"

Something warm and wicked spread throughout her body.

Something, thanks to the events of earlier that morning, she recognized as lust. Something she wanted to feel again with Robert. "Do you mind if I stay for a visit?"

Robert looked at her with knowing eyes. *Am I that obvious?* Before she could move one blue slipper, he stood and sauntered toward her, his eyes riveted to hers, and she tingled everywhere. As though he'd been doing this forever, he pulled her with his good arm, buried his face in her neck, and inhaled deeply. "You smell divine. Is that roses?"

Tilting her head to give him better access to the curve of her neck, she answered, "Yes."

"I will never see or smell roses again without thinking of you."

"Thank you."

After placing a kiss on her neck, he palmed her cheek with his free hand and smiled at her. "You look beautiful. Too beautiful for a man like me."

Covering his warm, large hand with hers, she stared into his eyes. "For a man like you? *No, for you.*"

He moaned and took her lips with his. Gentle and reverent. He kissed her forehead, each cheek. "You have ruined me for anyone else." His lips met hers again and the tempo changed. His tongue swept inside her mouth and he devoured her. Her arms wrapped around his neck, and she leaned into the kiss until every inch of her body pressed against every inch of his.

"What the hell..."

Robert and Mary jumped apart at the sound of her brother's harsh voice. "Spencer," Mary said, her voice shaking along with her body. The sensual feelings from her embrace with Robert vanished, replaced with embarrassment and panic. "You are days early." Behind them stood a young female servant who looked at her with wide eyes and a knowing smile before she turned and left.

"And fortunate that I am."

"Easy, Spencer," his wife Miranda said as she settled her hand on his forearm. "They were kissing, not in bed."

"How do we know they didn't just tumble out of it." He glared at Smythe. "And Mary is utterly ruined."

Smythe bellowed, "See here, Spencer."

Tears burned Mary's eyes and she wrapped her arms across herself, hoping to stop the violent trembling of her body. Robert, seeing her predicament, wrapped his arm over her shoulder and held her close.

Spencer cocked a brow, then narrowed his eyes, staring daggers at Robert. "Move away from her. You better hope Amesbury's servants are loyal and not gossips because that is the only thing keeping me from strangling you right now. I'm hoping you haven't ruined her for good. I highly doubt Mary would be happy living in the country as a spinster for the remainder of her days."

Mary gasped. "You wouldn't..." She pulled away from Robert and rushed to Miranda, grabbing both her hands in hers. "Please, you can't let him ruin my life. Robert loves me and I love him. We will marry."

Chilling laughter from her brother sent icicles up her spine, and she turned to face him. "I thought you cared about me?"

"Mary." Spencer inhaled and exhaled, and she could see him try to reel in his furry. "You know better than to question me about that. I blame myself. Obviously, I missed the warning signs about the feelings between you two. Of course, for the life of me, I can't imagine how it happened. As far as I know, you two only met once. Perhaps I gave Smythe too much leeway. Treating him like a friend instead of the hired runner that he is."

"Why cannot he be both?" Mary cried. "Why can he not be my husband?"

"Mary, it is not done. You are the granddaughter of a countess. A member of the aristocracy. If you were to marry him, you would be shunned."

"How do you know?" Miranda chimed in.

His fingers raked through his hair and he groaned. "My dear wife, because it is so. Now if you ladies would leave, I would like a word alone with Smythe. Oh, Miranda, find Aunt Violet and meet me in the drawing room where we first waited for Amesbury, who is among the missing with my other sister. God knows what the two of them are engaged in?"

Miranda escorted Mary to her room, hugged her tight and whispered, "I'll see what I can do. But I must say when your cousin, the Earl of Bridgeton, was accused of murdering his brother and his brother's pregnant wife and was shunned for twelve years, Spencer worried every day for him. He saw first-hand what the *ton* can do to one of their own during a scandal."

"I'm not accused of murder. I kissed a man. A man I love. And it's not as though we were caught during a function attended by hundreds."

"No. But servants gossip even worse. Even out here in the country word spreads like wildfire. That young servant who escorted us to Smythe's room, after we asked for you, knew you were alone with him. Already there is gossip." Miranda released her and left.

Mary was crestfallen, her legs so heavy they barely carried her to the bed where she curled on her side and let the tears flow. She would not regret her actions or her feelings for Robert—only that she couldn't speak to her brother before he found out. Robert may not be a privileged member of the *ton,* but he was more loyal and a gentleman than most of the eligible gentlemen she met at balls and soirees. They would just as likely persuade her out to the gardens to steal kisses and more for no other reason than they wanted to, regardless if they had any feelings for her. Rakes, many of them, who cared for nothing but themselves.

As the doorman closed the door behind them, Edward watched with pleasure as Elizabeth lifted her skirts and hurried up the staircase. The butler approached. "Mr. and Mrs. Spencer await you in the green drawing room."

As he strolled down the hall, he adjusted his own riding clothes and smoothed his hair. As he approached the closed double doors, he paused to wipe the sensual grin off his face and replace it with a friendly smile.

He stepped inside the room and paused. Something was wrong...or not right. Violet sat on the settee with Miranda. Violet looked positively ill and Miranda only slightly less ill. But it was Spencer who attracted his attention. Spencer was an affable fellow who joked and smiled often. Not today. Just in the few moments since he entered the room the man downed two fingers of whiskey and re-poured another. Edward pulled at his hastily tied cravat and knew without a doubt he and Elizabeth had been found out.

"I can explain."

Spencer swung his eyes toward Edward and raised one brow. "The devil you say? You were off riding with Elizabeth when it happened under this roof. So how can you?"

He had him there. If it wasn't about what happened between Elizabeth and him, then what? Even before Spencer spoke, he had a premonition of what occurred. Only before Spencer could speak Violet cried out, "I'm sorry. Ever since we were attacked I've felt ill. My duties as chaperone were lacking. It's all my fault Mary will be ruined. I failed you Spencer and I'm sorry." She sniffed most unladylike. "I will understand if you want to banish me from your home and family."

Miranda patted her aunt's hand. "Nonsense, you will always be part of this family." Miranda glared at her husband, willing him to argue. "Right, my dear, husband?"

Spencer looked uncomfortable and tugged at his cravat. "Yes. Violet is always welcome in this family, and I'm sorry I took my anger and frustration out on you." He went to help himself to more whiskey and Edward interrupted, "Perhaps Miranda could ring for a tea tray. You must be famished after your travels."

Spencer glared at him but put the decanter of whiskey down and began to pace the room. "I should've known from experience," he cleared his throat, "not my own of course, that ladies and gentlemen will...when they are attracted to each other...do things..." He groaned. "Bugger all, forget I said anything. I sound like someone's strict, hard-hearted father."

Spencer pierced Edward with his eyes and gesticulated toward him. "Did you know Mary and Smythe had feelings for each other?"

Edward choked then coughed as he hurried to pour himself a drink. After downing it and stifling another cough he turned to face Spencer. "I did not."

"Mary and Smythe were caught in a compromising position," Spencer said. "Would you please speak to your servants and try to keep them from discussing this if possible. I would like to muzzle the scandal and keep my sister's name pristine. Then, if you don't mind, I would like to discuss this matter in private with my family."

"If you require anything...anything at all, pull the bell pull and someone will attend to your needs." He bowed and left, closing the doors behind him. He paused just outside the large heavy double doors and breathed to calm his runaway heart. Poor Smythe and Mary. It would've been better if the scandal was about Elizabeth and he.

SLEEP PULLED at Mary when a light knock sounded on her door and her sister's voice asked, "May I come in?"

"Yes." Sitting up, Mary wiped the tears from her cheeks, stood, and met her sister halfway to the door and threw her arms around Elizabeth. "I'm so glad you're back from your ride. Spencer's here," she said between great big sobs robbing her lungs of air.

"I just saw Edward out in the hall, and he told me what happened." Elizabeth rubbed her back. "Easy. Don't cry. We'll think of something to make it all right."

"How?" Mary stepped back, swiped the tears from her face, and took a deep breath. "How?" she asked again.

Her sister looked puzzled. "I don't know. But when Spencer calms down he'll come up with a solution to this peccadillo. Meanwhile, he spoke to Edward and asked him to speak with his servants and see about squelching the gossip before it reaches beyond these walls. If he can do that, the problem of you being ruined is solved."

"Truthfully, that is not what upsets me most. I want to be with Robert. I want to marry him and he me." Mary's tears dried up and anger settled inside her. Anger at her brother for being so careless with her heart. She'd finally found someone worthy of giving it to. And he loved her back.

"Spencer wants to see us both," Elizabeth said with concern etched on her face. "Are you ready to face him again?"

Mary's shoulders slumped. "Might as well get it over with."

They entered the drawing room cautious and quietly.

Mary and Elizabeth sat on either side of Miranda on the settee while Violet sat looking horrified on a green and pink damask print chair facing them. Spencer stood, back ramrod straight, shoulders tense, staring into the flames in the hearth. Mary cleared her throat, letting her brother know she wanted him to speak and get her chastising over with.

At the sound, he pivoted around and shocked her by sitting in the chair next to Violet opposite the settee and looking almost apologetic. *Almost.* He definitely looked tired and harried with dark circles beneath his eyes and stress lines around his mouth.

"Mary, I'm not going to lecture you about what society expects of its members of the *ton.* You know the rules and etiquette better than I probably do. And God knows I broke many of them. But fortunately for me, I am a man and we are expected to break the rules. Not so for women. You must act most proper at all times or be subject to ridicule, gossip, and ruin. Not fair, I know, but such is our life." Spencer sat back and sighed deeply, looking as though he wished he were anywhere but there. "I have sent Mr. Smythe back to London."

Mary gasped but swallowed the words she wished to say to her brother.

"I had to for your own good. If by some miracle Amesbury can keep his servants from gossiping, then all should be well and your name, once again, will be surmountable to goodness and propriety. If not, then we must face the assault to your person head-on. And just so you haven't forgotten, servants have a gossip chain that works faster than any members of polite society. So while we sit here awaiting Amesbury to join us with his findings, I want you to tell me about you and Mr. Smythe and when it started."

Mary squirmed in her seat knowing all attention was on her and her transgressions. Surely he could not mean her to explain... She took a deep breath for courage and forged on. "We met for the first time when both you and he were injured when Violet and Miranda were taken by Mr. Baker. It was only Elizabeth and I home, besides Grandmother and Mother and the servants. Elizabeth and I both decided she would look after you and I would take care of Mr. Smythe."

"I see," Spencer said as he leaned forward, his elbows resting on his thighs, looking intently at her, waiting for more.

"I took care of him. When he woke up we spoke. Not for long, but enough to realize there was something pulling us together. Is pulling us together."

"You could have been ruined then. After that day, have you been sneaking off to see him? Sending notes back and forth? Did he come into our house at night?"

"No." She took offense at the implications. "I didn't see him until we left for here."

Spencer raised his brows in disbelief and her stomach suddenly became queasy. It would not do for her to cast up her accounts on Amesbury's lovely oriental rug.

"It's the truth. I may have daydreamed about him and wished to see him, but I didn't." Her eyes went to her hands clasped together in her lap. "I wanted to send him notes, but I didn't have the courage too."

"Good. If we can keep this situation from becoming scandalous, when we arrive back in London, I will actively seek a husband for you. I will invite several gentlemen, those I think worthy, to a small formal dinner party with of course other single ladies. We don't want to appear obvious."

"You...you." Mary's insides froze in disbelief. "You want to parade me in front of these eligible gentlemen—or more accurately—serve me up on a platter to the first who asks for my hand."

"Mary," Miranda interjected, "that is not true."

She swung her head and looked at Miranda. Even though she was angry tears burned her eyes. "Yes, it is."

"Mary," Spencer said, his voice several octaves lower than normal. "I know it sounds terrible, but this happens in homes all over England and beyond. I will do my best to keep anyone who attends from thinking you are desperate."

She gasped.

Spencer jumped up and paced the room. "Do you think I want to do this? Marry you to someone you do not love? Well I do not. But what choice have you given me?" He stood in front of her, dropped to his knees, and took her hands in his. "Please, this is not what I want for you."

She tried to yank her hands out of his, but he held on tight. "Then don't."

"I have to. I can't risk your reputation. Go get a good night's sleep as we leave first thing in the morning."

CHAPTER EIGHT

WHEN THE ONLY TWO PEOPLE LEFT IN THE DRAWING ROOM were Miranda and Spencer, Spencer stared out the window as darkness fell. "Am I wrong?" He forced the words out as a lump the size of his fist clogged his throat.

He heard the bustle of skirts and then his wife's arms circled his waist, her head rested against his back. "That is a difficult question to answer, since I'm a woman whose father once rejected the love of her life's offer of marriage. We may be together now, but look how many years were wasted living in pain, pining for the one who owned our hearts. I'm afraid, even after Mary is married, she will yearn for Mr. Smythe. I pray not, and she will come to love the man she marries, but we can't pretend to know how the future will unfold."

"It's so bloody complicated." Spencer pivoted around, enfolded Miranda in his arms, and rested his forehead lightly against hers. "I don't want her to think I'm heartless."

"She doesn't."

"No? I sounded heartless. I can't believe the words coming out of my mouth. I respect Smythe, but I can't give

Mary to him. It wouldn't be fair to her. Besides, Grandmother would never forgive me."

Miranda cupped his cheeks and smiled. "I believe in my heart all will work out for Mary." She raised on tiptoes and kissed him gently. His wife had such a gentle soul until someone threatened her or someone she loved, then the tiger in her showed her claws. He loved that about her and so much more. She'd been to hell and back and survived. Something Spencer had a hard time forgiving her dead father for. Thank God they belonged to each other now, and he would spend the rest of his days showing her how much he wanted, needed, and loved her.

He groaned and deepened the kiss, his tongue tangled with hers, his hands splayed across her back pulling her tight against him, letting her know how much he wanted her.

"Spencer, not here."

"Let us retire for the evening. I'll order a dinner tray sent to our room."

ROBERT SHOULD'VE NEVER TOUCHED Mary. He'd known she was above his station in life. But he couldn't control his heart. Of all the women in his life, why did he have to fall in love with her? Cruel, the fates were cruel. He wished they'd never met. Accept for the night she'd cared for him, became his angel, saved his life. And he truly believed she had saved him. Infection had ravaged his body from a filthy knife wound, and one day in her care he crawled back from the brink of death. Her voice—her essence—pulled him back from the darkness trying to swallow him.

He remembered it all even though he wasn't in his right mind. When his fever had broken and he saw her for the first time, he'd swear she glowed with a halo. Although why God sent an angel to him, with all the horrible things he'd done for his job and to survive in St. Giles as a young boy, baffled him.

His hands were soiled from death. He wasn't worthy of touching her with poisoned hands. So why had he done so? Because he believed they could overcome the differences in their stations. The question plagued him on the long ride back to London on horseback. He'd wanted to ride straight through, but the burning, stabbing pain down his injured side wouldn't relent. He'd forgone the sling, and if the warmth against his skin was any indication, he'd begun to bleed.

He stopped at a coaching station about eight hours outside of London. The innkeeper supplied fresh cloth. Inside his room, he removed his bandages, hissing loudly at the pain. What he wouldn't give for Mary's gentle touch. Using fresh water from the basin he cleaned off the blood and rewrapped his wounds and went in search of food.

After eating a bowl of stew made with meat he could not decipher and a piece of crusty bread in the public room, he sat at the table alone and downed several ales until his mind had trouble focusing on Mary and all he'd lost. Unfortunately, once he retired to his small room, all memories of her crashed back into focus, and he spent the night tossing and turning until he finally gave up sleeping and left before sunrise for the last eight grueling hours to London. Grueling because he knew his mind and heart would be with Mary. The only relief he received from his anguish was knowing Spencer would only marry Mary off to someone worthy of her. Someone possessing integrity and intelligence. Someone without vices, hidden secrets, or cruelty.

Once whispers of a suitor's name traveled to his ears, he would investigate, leaving no stone unturned until he came up with something incrementing or nothing at all. If he found nothing in the gentleman's past, he would resign himself to her marriage to another and wish them both well. If he found something damaging, he would send news of it to Spencer. He knew he had no hope to be with Mary, but damn if he would see her shackled to an unworthy and cruel man.

AFTER HELPING her sister into bed and waiting until she fell asleep, with tears staining her cheeks, Elizabeth made her way to her room, her heart heavy. Poor Mary. She tried to put herself into her sister's slippers and wondered what it would be like if Spencer refused Amesbury's request for her hand and married her to someone else? Unimaginable pain and heartache would paralyze her. She would want to die. Would never speak to her brother again.

Her hand flew to her chest as though her heart was being ripped out. Was that how Mary felt? No doubt it was and more. Elizabeth's sympathies lay with Mary, but also with Spencer. The pressure on him to make good and honorable matches for his sisters, she knew weighed heavily on his shoulders. She also knew he wanted love matches for them. Something not high priority with members of the *ton* but important to Spencer since he'd held out for love.

Perhaps Mary would come to love the man she married. Spencer would not marry her to just anyone. Elizabeth expected the most honorable gentlemen at the dinner party. At the moment, Elizabeth's brain refused to work on coming up with any eligible young men for Mary. There had to be several. She probed her brain and did come up with three. Mr. Philip Percy, eldest and only son to one of the richest, untitled families of the *ton*. His parents had both recently died and left him to raise two younger sisters. No doubt why he'd entered the marriage mart. He needed a wife to help him introduce his sisters into society. Elizabeth had danced with him a time or two during the beginning of the Season. He'd appeared affable enough, if not a little shy, and pleasant to look at. He never made a social call to their residence though. Didn't mean she couldn't talk to Spencer about inviting him.

On to another man whose face popped into Elizabeth's mind, Peter Jeffries, the Viscount Dayton. Elizabeth put his age around five and thirty. Not too old for Mary. His older brother had died from fever at a young age, moving Peter next in line to the earldom. If she recalled, his father had passed several years ago from a heart ailment. His mother still lived as well as one sister who'd married the Viscount Chapman. Dayton had a reputation for being a rake, but so had Wentworth, Myles, and Spencer. Perhaps there was some truth to the saying that reformed rakes made the best husbands. Elizabeth was hoping since Amesbury had the same reputation, although he didn't seem the least bit rakish now.

The last name was a long shot, a gentleman so secretive, Elizabeth knew little about him except he had entered the marriage market. The Duke of Newbury. He'd fought with Wellington in Waterloo and was a war hero. Some said he still worked for the War Office. He'd recently become a Duke when a distant cousin died having produced no heirs. Other than that Elizabeth knew nothing about him. Not his age or what he looked like, although she'd heard he'd sustained injury serving the Crown. Couldn't hurt to have a duke attend the dinner party. Going to the mahogany desk in her room, she took parchment and quill and scribbled down the three names to give to Spencer.

Just as Elizabeth finished writing the last name, a light knock on her door drew her attention. Who could that be at this late hour? Her hands went to the belt on her robe, making sure it was tied securely. "Who is it?" she whispered.

"Edward."

She gasped, opened the door, and pulled him inside,

poked her head into the hallway and scanned the darkness. The last thing Elizabeth needed was to cause another scandal for her brother to solve. She eased the door closed with the softest click and turned to Edward. "You shouldn't be here."

He hit her with a lopsided grin. "I know." Then he turned serious. "I was worried about you. We never had a chance to talk after we got back from our ride." His hands ran up and down her arms, and warm heat curled around her heart. "I wanted to see for myself that you are not upset about what we...did... That you are not still hurting."

A smile broke out on her lips at the blush staining Edward's cheeks. "Do you know how handsome you are when you blush?"

His blush deepened.

"Men don't blush." He scoffed.

Elizabeth leaned forward and kissed his cheek. "Oh yes, they do."

He captured her lips for a drugging kiss that sent all thought from her mind. When he pulled away and stepped back, so they were no longer touching, she moved forward, reached out for him, causing him to shake his head. "No. If we kiss again I won't be able to leave. I just needed reassurance about today...that you didn't regret it."

Unease tried to invade Elizabeth's mind and she buried it. She would not question whether Edward regretted making love to her. It would destroy her. The words blurted out regardless. "Do you?"

Reaching out, he pulled her back into his arms and buried his head in her hair. "No. It's possibly one of the only things in my life I don't regret. Which brings me to something I want to discuss with you." He stepped back once again. "I had planned on asking Spencer for your hand when we return to London, and before you say anything, I'm returning with you tomorrow. But with Mary and what is happening, I think we should wait. I don't want us to add to her pain."

If Elizabeth could love him any more than she already did, she would. How thoughtful of him. And horrible of her for not thinking about Mary's feelings regarding her and Edward's betrothal. "Thank you. You are most kind to think of my sister."

"Goodnight, my love." Silently he slipped out the door, and she took a shaky breath and hugged her tingling body. May his voice and him calling her love, always have that effect on her.

She tried to sleep, she really did, knowing the next two days would be long and tiresome. Visions of Edward making love to her out in the wildflower field with the sun kissing their skin invaded her mind. Not that Elizabeth minded, she wanted to remember. Never had she imagined it would be so pleasurable. That her body and mind would experience so many emotions fighting for recognition at the same time. The pain Elizabeth had heard about and worried about was minimal. Perhaps when you were with the one you loved it eased the hurt.

There was soreness down there, and she bled a little still, but she couldn't wait to make love with Edward again. Now Elizabeth understood why Spencer and Miranda spent so much time in their chambers at all hours of the day. And took dinner trays some nights instead of joining the family in the dining room. They were, after all, newly married. She couldn't wait until her marriage to Edward.

THE EMPTY CRYSTAL glass hung from Spencer's fingers as he sat in a wingback chair in front of the heart in their bedchamber while Miranda sat at her dressing table brushing her long red tresses. He'd drank more than his share of brandy and would regret it on the morrow. But bloody hell, he needed to vanish the look on Smythe's face when he threw him out of Cliff House. He'd accepted his fate with honor, not fighting him on it, which made Spencer admire the bloke even more. But Smythe's eyes couldn't hide the pain, the anguish torturing him.

Then Mary. He thrust one hand into his hair, tugging until he winced in pain. Mary—his quiet, soft spoken, shy sister. Seeing her face contort with pain, her eyes wild with glassy tears, and her body collapse in on itself haunted him. Spencer had broken her. Broken her body, heart, and soul. He raised the glass to drink. Finding it empty, he threw it against the fireplace and reveled in hearing it crash into broken shards. Shattered like Smythe's and Mary's hearts.

His wonderful wife climbed on his lap and hugged him to her breast. She always knew what he needed before he did. "You know I don't agree with your decision about Mary and her man, but I support you nonetheless. I'm not in your boots, but I understand you have her best interest in mind. As her brother you want the best for her. The best marriage, the best gentleman and happiness. And if not love within the marriage, at least a mutual respect and honor."

Spencer wrapped his arms around Miranda and breathed in her scent belonging to her alone. She'd always smelled like jasmine and it soothed him. Soothed his nerves, his mind and soul. At times like this it was hard to believe they went twelve years without each other. Twelve years pining for the other. He'd been broken and never knew it. First he thought himself in love with Sofia LaFleur and then Lady Isabella Seabrook. When in truth he hated the first woman and loved Bella as a friend. He and Bella had a special relationship, even now, that most couldn't understand. How could a man and woman be best of friends? Well, the answer was yes. They didn't see each other as often since she'd married Myles and he Miranda, but that didn't lesson their friendship. And after going to Miranda with something, then to his cousin Bridgeton, Bella was the next in line. God love his wife for understanding. Myles...well...he didn't understand and probably never would.

"I'm sorry."

Miranda hugged him tighter. "For what?"

"For being an arse today and wallowing in my cups."

"Isn't that what men do when they can't face situations they don't like or can't control," she teased.

"I will speak for all men when I say no. We don't need our spirits or time pondering the situation alone in our studies." It was a lie, of course, but his wife knew that.

"No apologizes necessary. I love you, flaws and all." More teasing from his lovely bride.

"How did I ever get so lucky to marry you?"

"It wasn't luck that brought us together."

Sudden sadness in Miranda's eyes had Spencer regretting his words. After Miranda's father rejected his suit of her because of family scandal involving his cousin, Bridgeton, Miranda had disappeared for many years. During those years her Aunt Violet's third husband raped Miranda, stole money and left them in the country. Aunt Violet and Miranda traveled to London this past spring for the Season because it was high time Miranda married and money was scarce. He thanked God every day that they did. It brought them back together, even if the circumstances were horrendous. Violet's husband had come back during the spring, kidnapped both her and Miranda and tortured them. Smythe and his runners found them. There was that name again...Smythe.

He owed the runner everything. Guilt sliced through him, he gasped, and jerked almost sending Miranda to the floor. "Sorry."

"You caught me, that's all that matters." Climbing off his lap she held out her hand with a shy smile. "Come to bed."

Sleep would elude him he knew, but when his lovely wife wanted to go to bed with him, never, ever, would he refuse. He held her close to his heart beneath the coverlet and listened to her breathing as it slowed and evened out while sleep overtook her. He held her that way the entire night as he questioned his decisions of the day. And asked himself, who was he to play with two people's lives, hearts, and future happiness?

FOR THE LONG day on the road, Mary barely uttered a word to anyone. She jostled in the carriage next to Elizabeth, staring out the window, wishing she saw Robert riding outside protecting them as on the way there. Instead she saw Amesbury and Spencer. She knew they would be safe with two outriders on the back of the coach as well, but she wanted Robert. Then she chided herself. It was time to toughen up and realize a future with him would not happen. She would marry some aristocrat. A man her brother handpicked. And Mary knew her brother would only choose someone worthy of her. Her marriage wouldn't have love, but it wouldn't be terrible. She would never love another, Robert held her heart, but she would force herself to be content. The children she would bare would fill her heart to bursting. Everything would be well. It was easy to tell her mind, but her heart cracked wide open at the thought.

Elizabeth reached for her hand. "We are nearly home. Are you ready?"

Ready? Could anyone truly be ready when their future lay in the hands of another. Mary could lie to herself and say none of this bothered Spencer, but it did. He couldn't look her in the eye, and he'd been in a foul mood since they left Cliff House. But she couldn't bear to feel sorry for him—he could choose Robert for her.

Miranda and Aunt Violet sat opposite her, both looking sympathetic to her cause. Then Mary thought of her grandmother, the Dowager Countess of Bridgeton and her mother. Would her brother tell them? She didn't believe so. She prayed not, she didn't want to disappoint her grandmother, who had practically raised her since their mother lay in bed most days with one ailment or another. No, she didn't want to see displeasure on her grandmother's face.

Her hand being squeezed by Elizabeth forced her out of her woolgathering. "As ready as I can be." Mary's next words addressed her sister-in-law. "Did Spencer say anything about word reaching London about me? And when will this dinner party will be held?"

Miranda's compassionate eyes met hers. "As far as we know, Amesbury squelched the servant's gossip and no word of what transpired reached London. As for the invitations, I will hurry to get the them out tomorrow. Five days should be doable. Is there a gentleman you would like to invite?"

Her lungs ached. They burned as if on fire as she tried to breathe. "No. I'll leave the list to my brother." She tightened her hand around her sister's then let go and told herself not to cry. Crying wouldn't solve anything. Although the first thing Mary planned on doing once she reached the sanctity of her chamber was to expel her heartbreak with fresh tears. And then never allow herself to repeat it and accept her future. The future Spencer would choose for her. She could be brave. She would be brave.

CHAPTER NINE

THE NIGHT OF THE FORMAL DINNER, MARY'S LADIES' MAID, Lucy, dressed her in a lovely high waist, dark blue silk gown with light blue lace overlay and dark blue flowers embroidered in several repeating rows near the hemline. Matching dark blue ribbon tied beneath her chest drew one's attention to the low scooped neckline exposing a swelling of creamy breast. Oh, the amount was proper, but she felt exposed. She once loved this gown. Tonight she felt on the auction block at Tattersalls.

The talented fingers of her maid styled her hair, curling it and pinning it up with curls wound in blue ribbon cascading down around her left shoulder. Even she had to admit she looked beautiful. A family of butterflies took flight inside her stomach, and she fought the urge to hug her belly. She could do this. What was about to happen tonight happened in drawing rooms and dining rooms all across England and other countries. All Mary had to remember was her brother wouldn't marry her to an ogre, someone too old or too young. She needed to have faith in Spencer. As she descended the stairs, leading down to the grand foyer, her hands gripped the mahogany bannister as a lifeline, and she whispered the word, "Faith."

She knew she was early, the guests wouldn't arrive for another fifteen minutes, but she wanted to settle herself in the lovely burgundy and rose drawing room. Upon entering, thinking she would be alone, surprise hit her when she glimpsed Spencer standing stiff and tall in front of a large window, his arms linked together behind his back.

"Are you ready for this evening?"

How had he known it was her? "Yes."

Pivoting around, her brother's eyes took her in. "You look beautiful. I know this is not what you want, but I thank you."

Tears swam in Mary's eyes, she used her gloved hands to soak them up before they could escape. Words eluded her and thankfully, Miranda and Aunt Violet entered the room, saving her from replying. Thank goodness Grandmother and Mother were in the country because this night would be hard enough. Not to mention how would Spencer explain to them the sudden need to marry her off? Her stomach recoiled. Food would not go down easy tonight.

Miranda acknowledged her first. "You look stunning, my dear." She kissed her cheek. "I'd hug you but we mustn't wrinkle our gowns."

"You look lovely. Green is your best color with your hair and eyes." Mary complemented.

The butler entered, bowed and announced the arrival of her cousin, Bridgeton, and his countess, Amelia, and the Duke of Wentworth and his sister, Lady Penelope Seabrook.

Her insides finally settled—family and friends. No single gentlemen...yet. Mary greeted the new arrivals, wondering what was keeping Elizabeth. She curtsied. "Your Grace, how nice to see you again."

"Lady Mary." He bowed over her hand. "I wouldn't want to be anywhere else tonight. Your Grace sends her regards— she is unable to attend." He acknowledged his sister. "You remember Lady Penelope."

Mary curtsied. "Yes. It is a pleasure to see you again."

Lady Penelope curtsied and smiled. "I'm looking forward to this evening. Perhaps we will have time to chat."

"Yes, I would like that very much."

The Seabrook family had only recently learned about Penelope's existence. She was the natural born daughter of the previous duke and his mistress. Wentworth, with his mother's blessing, introduced Penelope into society recently as his sister and none, but a very few, dared cross the powerful duke and question her parentage or the use of the title lady. Mary wondered if being rich and marrying into the family of a duke would make some eligible gentleman of the *ton* ignore the circumstances of her birth. Mary wished her luck and hoped she found her happily-ever-after. Mary looked forward to getting to know her better. She was terribly shy and utterly beautiful with her blonde hair and blue eyes resembling her brother, the duke.

Bridgeton approached her. "Do you not have a hug for your favorite cousin."

Mary hugged Bridgeton carefully, not wanting to crush her dress or his exquisite charcoal coat or silver paisley waist coat, not to mention his white shirt and starched cravat tied expertly. "How handsome you look this evening, cousin."

"And you, my dear cousin, are positively radiant."

Amelia, his countess, chimed in, "No hugs for us, after all the work our maids went into pressing our gowns." She took both Mary's hands into hers. "William is right, you do look radiant. Has one of the single gentlemen invited tonight captured your heart?"

Hiding her pain and anguish proved an impossible task.

Mary noticed Amelia saw it right away, linked her arm with hers, and led her to the side of the room. "My dear, is something amiss?"

"I'm sorry." Mary blinked and willed her tears to dry up. "There is someone, but Spencer won't allow it."

Amelia squeezed her hand. "Why ever not?"

"If I confide in you, you must promise not to tell Bridgeton."

"One thing I learned early on in my relationship with your cousin is that we don't keep secrets. Perhaps if I confide in him, he will speak to Spencer on your behalf. You do remember when Wentworth refused to allow anything to pass between William and me. Even had him thrown in Newgate for attempting to murder me, which of course, he did no such thing."

How could she forget the tragic events leading up to the marriage between her cousin and his young bride, only several years older than Mary. "This is different. He is not a member of the peerage. Far from it."

"Indeed." Amelia hid her shock well. "Still, there is always hope. Oh dear, your cousin is glancing this way with a look I know all too well. I will do what I can even without the gentleman's name."

Finally, Mary spotted Elizabeth entering the room on the arm of Amesbury. No doubt she'd been waiting for him to arrive. Perhaps tonight they would announce their betrothal. She wanted nothing but happiness for her sister, even though her heart ached for her own betrothal and happiness to Robert. Several more guests entered the drawing room as she stood in a quiet corner all alone. Two gentlemen she recognized as Mr. Philip Percy and the Viscount Dayton were announced by the butler. Neither had shown any interest in either Elizabeth or her during the Season. What was Spencer thinking inviting them? Also announced was an old matron,

Lady Southfork, and her granddaughter, Lady Julia Finley. Obviously Spencer needed to make an even number of gentlemen and ladies. He'd chosen well because Lady Julia was gracious, not gossipy, boring, or frivolous. It was her third Season. Perhaps she would catch the eye of one of gentlemen in attendance.

The next gentleman to arrive was The Duke of Newbury. Mary had never seen him before, nor heard of him. Her insides turned to stone at the sight of him. She would place his age around twenty-nine or thirty, but other than that words escaped her. Her eyes, however, were riveted to the poor, unfortunate man. He leaned heavily on a cane, his left leg appeared not to bend at the knee. A black patch covered one eye, making him resemble a pirate. A red, raised scar that ran from mid-cheek to across his chin looked new and decorated the same side as the patch. Fortunately, for him, he had one uninjured side, which made him almost handsome in a hard sort of way. Where on earth had Spencer found the Duke? More to the point, had he known about his shortcomings? Mary prided herself in not being petty or selfish or putting too much stock in a person's looks. In the Duke's case, even she may find it hard to overlook his disfigurement.

"I know what you're thinking," Miranda said as she joined her. "You are wondering how your brother chose his guest list? I can assure you he spent hours agonizing over it with Elizabeth and myself. The three invited are actively seeking wives and from what he could deduce, they are honorable men, although Spencer couldn't find out much about the duke, except he served in the war with Wellington and fought alongside him at Waterloo. Some say he is a hero. His Grace came to London only recently after inheriting from a distant cousin. The poor man. I don't believe Spencer knew he was a cripple." Miranda wrapped her arm through Mary's. "Come, let us go to your brother and get the introductions over with."

Her feet, weighed down by invisible stones, shuffled along beneath her skirt. Vibrations invaded all her muscles. Even though her lungs expanded and contracted she didn't think she took in air or expelled any, nor did her heart appear to beat.

"Ah, here is one of my lovely sisters now," Spencer said. "Miss Mary Spencer, I would like to present His Grace, The Duke of Newbury."

The duke took her gloved hand with his free one and made an awkward bow while he brushed his lips across her knuckles. "The pleasure is all mine, Miss Spencer." The whole time his face appeared impassive, except for one second she thought she saw an amused look cross his features. She must have been mistaken.

She pulled her hand back trying to appear gracious and sincere as she curtsied. "You Grace, it is a pleasure to make your acquaintance." It deemed terribly hard not to stare at his horrible scar or black patch, but she thought she did well.

Viscount Dayton and Mr. Phillip Percy were introduced next. The other gentlemen bowed, took her hand, and pressed their lips to her knuckles. Too bad she felt nothing. Three kisses to her knuckles and not one single tingle.

Spencer looked at her with a silly grin on his face. What on earth was he up too? And then all air vacated her lungs and her knees threatened to buckle. Her shocked eyes moved back and forth between her brother and the newly arrived guest being introduced by the butler.

"A Mr. Robert Smythe."

It couldn't be? How? Never had she seen him dressed so fine. He looked every bit the part of a gentleman of society in his dark brown coat, tan waistcoat, brown breeches, brown

Hessians, white crisp linen shirt with a perfectly tied cravat. Dare she hope? Dream?

"Mr. Smythe," her brother said, "you remember my sister, Miss Spencer."

He bowed over her hand and pressed his lips to her knuckles, causing those elusive tingles. "Miss Spencer, it is a pleasure to see you again." A smile spread across her lips at the look of relief on his face and the twinkle in his creamy brown eyes.

"Very nice to see you again." So shocked she was, it was a wonder she could speak.

Before Mary could say anything more, Bridgeton and Wentworth joined them and took over the conversation. Elizabeth wrapped her arm with hers and led her away to the other side of the room. Was she to spend the entire evening watching from afar? Not a half hour ago she'd wanted to do just so, now her insides were alive, tingling with the need to socialize and enjoy the night ahead.

"Why did you drag me away?"

Elizabeth laughed. "Because you needed saving. If you could've seen the way you and Mr. Smythe were making eyes at each other. I almost opened my fan to cool my face. Lord, if any of the other single gentlemen in the room had hopes of winning your favors, their hopes have been squashed."

"I can't believe he's here? Does this mean? What made Spencer change his mind?" So many words so quickly caused breathlessness and her hand flew to her chest.

Soft laughter again from her sister. "I don't know the answer. A change of heart I suppose."

"Drat, dinner is announced. I'm too excited to eat anything," Mary exclaimed.

Mary found herself being escorted into the dining room by Mr. Percy. His mouth turned up into a bright smile at having the honor. Spencer and Miranda sat at each end of the long table. Mary was seated between Amesbury and Mr. Percy with Elizabeth on Amesbury's other side. Across from her was Mr. Smythe with Penelope on his right and the Duke of Newbury on Penelope's left. Lady Julia was seated on Smythe's left with Viscount Dayton on her right. Spencer had managed to put all the single people together in the middle of the table.

Perhaps tonight wouldn't be for not. Perhaps Penelope and Lady Julia would find suitors among the single men.

ROBERT COULD HARDLY BELIEVE the events of today, which began with him holding an invitation that arrived that morning. He'd read it three times before understanding the meaning. Well, it didn't take him three reads to ascertain he'd been invited to a formal dinner party at the home of Mr. Stuart Spencer. The reason it took three reads was disbelief. When the implication sank in, his heart beat regularly for the first time since he'd left Mary at Cliff House. Perhaps Spencer was allowing his suit of Mary. It could mean nothing else. What had changed the man's mind? And bugger all, did he have the proper clothing to attend?

Standing in the Spencer family drawing room now, glancing around at all the ladies and gents he realized his clothing, though not possessing the finest quality of cloth, looked passable enough. His old boots had polished up nicely. As a servant introduced him, he fought down panic threatening to overrun his entire being.

Thankfully, Wentworth and Bridgeton approached him, no doubt having witnessed his near panic, and welcomed him, putting him at ease. If one could be at ease as a guest at a polite society dinner party. Something he'd never expected to attend. He'd dreamed of a life with Mary but never expected it to come to fruition. Tonight, his heart soared with the knowledge it would happen. Why else would he be here?

When his eyes connected with Mary's, he couldn't look away. She looked breathtaking and beyond beautiful, making him wonder why she chose him when she could have any single gentleman in the room. And there were several if he wasn't mistaken.

Before he became acclimated to the drawing room, dinner was announced and to his utter disappointment he escorted Elizabeth into dinner and not Mary. However, as he found himself seated across from Mary, and would be able to look at her throughout the meal, he relaxed and the tension eased from his shoulders and neck. He'd once heard it was bad form to speak across the table, so he would wait until he witnessed someone else doing it before he did. Meanwhile, he made small talk with Lady Penelope. Thankfully, she didn't mention him being a Bow Street Runner.

Occupying the seat on Lady Penelope's other side sat a rather large, imposing and intimidating duke, possessing a nasty scar across his face, an eye patch, and a leg that appeared crippled. Fortunately for him he was a duke and not part of the working class. He'd starve in the lower classes of London before someone gave him a job. Smythe's curiosity had him wanting to ask about his injuries, knowing it was probably taboo had him keeping his mouth closed. Perhaps tonight was a test to ascertain if he could fit in with Mary's family and polite society in general. If it was, he would not fail.

His eyes fell upon Mary and she smiled and blushed. God, how he loved her. He wanted to say something, anything, but afraid to break etiquette rules, he sat there staring at her with what he knew was a stupid grin and a possessiveness he felt down to his very bones. She belonged to him.

Footmen began bringing food, at least he thought they

were footmen. The upper class had too many servant names. Doorman, footman, under-footman, butler... The first course, a pureed soup, smelled quite good even if he didn't know what ingredients were used. Before he dared pick up a utensil from the table, he looked across at Amesbury and followed his lead. Cloth napkin draped on lap. Even he knew to do that. What he didn't know was what spoon to use until Amesbury picked up his. He sighed with relief as he dipped his spoon into his soup and tried his hardest not to make slurping noises. The taste was odd, but not in a bad way.

Several more courses came and went and each time he waited for Amesbury to pluck a utensil off the table. The footman refilled his glass several times with wine, causing the room to tilt and the voices surrounding him to blend into a mess of non-sequential noise. No more wine for him, and he refused another refill. By the time sweetmeats, cheese, and assorted fruits were served, Smythe thought he'd burst through his breeches. He couldn't believe people ate like this on a daily basis.

All of a sudden, everyone stood. He promptly rose and watched as the ladies exited the room and the gentlemen resumed their seats as port and cheroots were passed around. Smythe did love a good smoke, but he passed on the port. It wouldn't do to get drunk and embarrass himself or Mary. He needed to keep his wits about himself. The conversation turned to politics, and he listened with an avid ear. He would never have a spot in the House of Commons, but that didn't stop him from keeping abreast of current government affairs. He listened but didn't utter a word.

Not long after, they rejoined the ladies in the drawing room. Bridgeton invited him to play chess. Thankfully he knew how and prided himself on being a moderately good player. After a rather good move, where he swiped

Bridgeton's knight off the board, his opponent said, "You're proficient at chess. When do you have time?"

"I find the time. I have a chess board in my office."

"I never noticed. I think you know why I asked you to play? Spencer wants me to talk with you about Mary and what your intentions are toward her?"

He'd thought his attentions were obvious after Spencer caught Mary and he in a private moment. "I would like to marry her."

"How do you propose to support her? I know you let rooms in a tenement in St. Giles. But Mary needs better lodgings."

Smythe fought the urge to tug on his cravat, which seemed to be getting tighter and tighter by the second. "I have money saved up. I will let a house in Cheapside. I would think living amongst doctors, bankers, and lawyers would be acceptable to Mr. Spencer."

Bridgeton kept his eyes on the board, contemplating his next move. "I believe that will be acceptable to my cousin. I know you will find the next question rude, but do you make enough money to sustain that address in the long-term."

He wanted to laugh. Did Bridgeton expect him to come right out and say how much blunt he made? He didn't believe so. "Yes. Between running the office of the Bow Street Runners and the work I pick up on the side, I do quite well, thank you."

"Christ." Bridgeton raised his eyes and looked apologetic. "This is damn awkward. One last question and then we can concentrate on the bloody game. Spencer has a family ring he would like to give you for Mary. It belongs to his mother, but he didn't want to insult you if you have a family ring of your own. Do you?"

"No. I would be honored to accept the ring on behalf of Mary."

"Good, good. I need a brandy, pardon me for a moment."
He stood and then paused. "Would you care for some?"

"Why not."

"Oh, and one more thing, Mary's dowry is five thousand
pounds." Bridgeton held up his glass. "The two of you should
do just fine."

CHAPTER TEN

AFTER MOST OF THE GUESTS LEFT, EXCEPT FOR Wentworth, Amesbury, and Bridgeton, the four men sat in Spencer's study enjoying a smooth, aged brandy.

"Do you think me allowing Mary and Smythe to marry will cause much of a scandal?" Spencer said as he took a healthy swallow of his drink.

Bridgeton answered before anyone could respond. "Most definitely. But since when can't this family deal with a little scandal. What I want to know is did you discuss this with Grandmother? Because the only approval you need is hers."

"I did. Sent a letter before we even left Cliff House." He shivered, thinking about her reply. "She wasn't pleased. Hoped both Elizabeth and Mary would marry into titles." He looked at Amesbury. "I can count on you asking for Elizabeth, can't I?"

Amesbury's nodded his head.

"Good. Because she said if I made an advantageous match for Elizabeth, Mary could marry Smythe. We all know the man is honorable and brave. But is he marriageable? Can he provide for Mary? Not that she doesn't come with a large dowry and a nice estate in Sussex, thanks to Grandmother, but still, Smythe is a proud man, will he want to rely on his wife's riches?"

"Many men do," Wentworth replied. "But I know what you mean. Have you had a conversation with him about his finances? Perhaps he's squirrelled away a large nest egg. Broach the subject with him." He cocked a brow. "You do need to have a private conversation with him to discuss particulars anyway so bring it up."

"It just so happens," Spencer cocked a brow back at his friend, "Bridgeton spoke with him this evening, I think most of my financial worries, where they will live and such, have been answered satisfactorily. But you are right, Wentworth, I still need to speak with him. Members of the *ton* discuss people's finances all the time. Nothing is secret when it comes to money within the realm. So I won't hesitate discussing money with Smythe."

"Nonsense," Amesbury interjected. "Society only knows what is entailed. Or if someone is stupid to shout their wealth from the rooftops, or they gamble it away. I challenge any of you to guess my worth?"

Spencer coughed. "We can discuss this when you ask for my sister's hand."

Amesbury grinned. "Certainly."

"Not to change the subject, but what do you think about Newbury for Penelope?" Wentworth asked, his attention focused into his crystal tumbler half full of amber liquid."

Spencer spoke up, "It appeared strange enough when Elizabeth came up with his name, but then you did as well, making me curious. Dayton and Percy I could understand, but Newbury?" He paused and tossed back his drink. "She may not want herself shackled to a cripple. And his scar is positively frightening. And the black patch. God knows what his eye looks like beneath that thing."

"Are you a sissy?" Bridgeton said with a smirk. "It's not as though you have to live with him and view his frightening scar, patch, and leg on a daily basis. Let Penelope decide."

"Actually," the duke drawled. "I will decide. I'm not saying I've set my sights on Newbury, but he's in the running. Besides, snagging a duke would be a *fait accompli* for my dear bastard of a sister."

"Will you not consider her feelings at all?" The earl asked, who not long ago had to prove his worth to Wentworth in order to wed his sister, Amelia. Wentworth had hated Bridgeton with a passion when they first met. Thankfully all ended well.

"Does Penelope know tonight was as much about her as it was Mary?" Spencer queried as he refilled his glass from the decanter, held it up offering refills."

Wentworth leaned forward, holding out his empty glass. "I never came right out and said anything. But I could tell by the way she was glaring at me over dinner she suspected as much. Tomorrow, I'll broach the subject and get her thoughts. She is only ten and seven, but with her background, I think it's best to marry her off as soon as possible. I'd hate to have her suffer through another Season. She did not attract favorable attention in the spring. The whispers and such. The *ton* is cruel. I'm torn also because she only recently came into our lives, and I don't want to lose her yet."

"Do you still see your sisters, Bella and Amelia." Bridgeton rose from his seat and took the decanter off Spencer's desk and refilled his and Amesbury's glass.

"Yes."

"There is your answer. You will still see her. Not daily, but truthfully there are times I think Amelia spends more time with her family than with me." Bridgeton took a large sip from his glass. "Damn, this is good brandy." Bridgeton grinned as he looked at His Grace.

"Hating you came easily when we first met," Wentworth griped. "I can revisit that."

Spencer, Amesbury, and Bridgeton chuckled, but it was Bridgeton who said, "As if Amelia or your duchess would allow it."

"Are you saying my wife wears the breeches when it comes to family affairs?" The duke looked appalled.

"I'm not commenting either way," Spencer said with a shoulder shrug.

Amesbury answered, "Well, I do remember a time when Emma..."

"Shut up." The duke growled, snagged the decanter off the desk and sloshed the liquid into his glass, glaring at Bridgeton. "Don't say a word. As I said already, I can hate you again."

Wisely Bridgeton remained silent, his expression amused.

After his friends left, Spencer found himself contemplating his future. Not necessarily his future but that of his sisters. He didn't want Mary to ever regret her decision to choose Smythe. It would break her heart if society shunned her, and she was forced to leave all she'd ever known behind. Or would it break his heart to witness his sister being shunned? Mary would probably be perfectly happy living on her Sussex Estate with Smythe who could take a job as the local constable. Would Smythe be happy leaving the cutthroats, drunks, thieves, and murderers behind in London? If he loved Mary, indeed he would be.

Since Miranda had come back into Spencer's life, he'd never been more content. Miranda completed him. He'd been a lost soul for years. It was hard to describe what loving her and receiving her love in return meant to him. Each morning he woke up with her head resting on his chest, causing his heart to flutter. Knowing the one he loved was by his side each day made him feel invincible. Made him feel as though anything were possible.

How could he get in the way of Mary or Elizabeth experiencing the same? Loving and being loved. No other greater joy existed in this vast world.

Amesbury. He didn't think Elizabeth would ever regret setting her sights on him. He'd admit there was a time he thought he wouldn't come up to scratch. Especially after the broken betrothal with Lady Beth. They were both fortunate that didn't cause more of a scandal and one or both of them were ruined. Most likely Lady Beth. Men had a way of being forgiven for bad and ungentlemanly behavior. Not gently bred ladies.

Damn, but they had two weddings to prepare for. Mary's first. A nice quiet ceremony in the country would suffice. The less attention to the nuptials the better. No sense feeding fuel to the gossips.

Elizabeth and Amesbury could marry where and when they wished. They only needed a small appropriate time between the two. Mary deserved her day, as did Elizabeth.

Perhaps after both weddings, he would take Miranda on an extended trip to the continent. Aunt Violet as well if she so chose. Perhaps Violet would find a nice, lonely gentleman to spend her elder years with.

CHAPTER ELEVEN

THE DAY OF MARY'S WEDDING FOUND THEM AT SPENCER House, her cousin Bridgeton's country estate, in Dover. Most of their family and friends were attending. Wentworth's neighboring estate, Stoney Cross Manor, had a lovely small stone chapel he'd offered for the nuptials. The same chapel Wentworth and his duchess, Emma, Bridgeton and his countess, Amelia, and Myles and his countess, Bella married in. To Mary's heart, she was being blessed and honored to exchange vows within the same ancient stone walls.

As Mary walked up the small, narrow aisle on Spencer's arm her heart pounded. Smythe's intense eyes never left her face, nor did the smile on his lips falter. He looked more handsome than she remembered. A week had gone by since she'd last set eyes on him. Seeing him now, sent her body aquiver and her heart soring. At the end of the aisle, Spencer kissed her on the cheek and whispered into her ear, "I'm so happy for you. Now you have your happily-ever-after as Miranda and I."

Tears pooled in her eyes and she blinked them away. "Thank you. I love you."

"I love you, too."

He removed her hand from his arm and held it out, offering her to Smythe. "Take care of my sister."

"I will."

Spencer took his seat on the bench with Miranda, their grandmother, and mother. Elizabeth, Violet, and Amesbury sat behind them.

The ceremony went quickly, at least Mary believed it did. She could barely hear the vicar's words over the pounding in her ears. Her eyes widened when they said their vows and exchanged rings. Smythe slipped her mother's delicate gold filigree, diamond, and emerald ring on her finger. Tears blurred her vision as she looked at her mother and mouthed the words, "Thank you." She was rewarded with a rare smile in return.

She slipped a gold band on Smythe's ring finger that she'd had made at a jewelers on Bond Street the day after the dinner party. After that night she knew Spencer would allow them to wed.

On the carriage ride back to Spencer House Smythe pulled her onto his lap and kissed her. Desire unfurled and spread heat throughout her body. She held onto his lapels, tilted her head, and kissed him with all the love and desire consuming her. He moaned, cupped her face, and deepened the kiss until they broke away breathless and gasping.

She laughed first and he joined her as their foreheads touched. "It's going to be a long couple of hours before we're alone," her new husband said as he brushed her lips with his.

"I know. Is it rude to skip one's wedding breakfast?" She smiled and muffled a nervous laugh.

"I believe it is. Which brings me to mind that Spencer said Bridgeton had rooms in the south wing prepared for us. He actually said it is far away from any other bed chamber and will be private. I almost choked. And I definitely blushed."

"Thank goodness, I was worried about tonight. But tomorrow we will travel to Sussex to my...no...our estate and spend a fortnight blessedly alone. Well, alone except for a minimal staff." She hugged him close. "I can't wait to show you the property. It is beautiful. I always knew I was going to inherit the estate from my grandmother, but I expected to wait until she passed. I'm shocked she gave it to me, to us, for a wedding present."

He nuzzled her neck and then moved her to sit on the seat beside him as they approached her cousin's estate. "To you. Your grandmother gave it to you, but I'm honored that you think of it as ours. I love you."

She rested her head on his shoulder and curled her arm through his. "You're welcome. Someday it will belong to our children."

He squeezed her thigh. "I can't wait to make babies with you." He cleared his throat. "I never thought this, being married to you, would ever come to fruition. I thought I would spend the rest of my life thinking and dreaming about you and hating the man lucky enough to win your hand. I have no words to describe how I feel that your family believes me worthy of you. I'm honored and astounded that you are my wife. That we get to spend the rest of our lives together. That I get to show you how much I love you every second, minute, and hour of every day. I'm not convinced I'm worthy of you, but I will try to be that man for you."

Tears clogged her throat, refusing to let words escape. How had she ever gotten so fortunate to deserve such love from this remarkable, strong, brave, and honorable man—and so much more. Men were afraid of him because of his size, demeanor, and determination to keep the streets of London safe for all. He fought for all classes. And somehow he fell in love with her. "I promise to be the best wife. To support you and try not to worry for your safety when you are working. Your work, keeping the streets safe, is your calling. I'll love and cherish our babies. And most importantly, I will love you until the end of time."

"I need a moment before we exit the carriage." He wiped moisture from his cheeks and cleared his throat. "Your entire family is waiting for us."

Mary leaned forward and looked out the window. "They are indeed." Her gloved fingers dried up her tears. "Are we ready?"

He tapped the roof and almost immediately the footman opened the door, lowered the steps. Smythe exited, held out his hand, and helped his bride down to the cheers of her family surrounding them and escorting them inside for the wedding feast. Mary's insides sang with delight. Never had she felt happier or more loved. She looked forward to Elizabeth and Amesbury's wedding next month. She wanted her sister to experience the same joy and elation.

The hours spent sitting around the table, eating, toasting with champagne, and listening to all the laughter and joy from her family and friends flew by. Before she knew it she was ascending the elaborate staircase in her cousin's home, her arm wrapped through her husband's. Mary's body hummed with nerves and anticipation. The night before her grandmother, not her mother, had visited her room and given her the marriage bed talk. Mary almost giggled out loud at the absurdity of the conversation. She loved Grandmother, but she was of an age when the less one knew about the marriage bed the better. All she had to say was submit to your husband's needs. There would be pain, but hopefully only one time. Hopefully? Did she refer to the fact that some husbands beat their wives?

Anyway, over the last several years Elizabeth and she had

learned much on their own of what occurred between husband and wife or mistress and protector. Grandmother spoke of several things but told her not to be afraid, it would make it more painful and possibly would anger her husband. Never. Mary would never be afraid of Robert, nor would he be angry with her if she was to become frightened from the intimacy of the bed.

"My love, we have arrived at our chambers." Robert raised their joined hands and kissed her gloved knuckles. "Your maid will arrive momentarily to help you."

"I'm sorry, I was woolgathering."

He opened the door and swept her up into his arms before she could protest. Once the door closed behind them, he lowered her to the floor and met her eyes with his compassionate ones. "Are you worried about consummating our marriage?" She loved it when her big, brave husband blushed.

"Only a little. Mostly I'm looking forward to it." Now her cheeks heated.

"Would you like to go into the dressing room and prepare?"

"How did you know there is a dressing room? You've never been in these rooms before."

The sound of him chuckling eased her nerves. "Spencer gave me a tour earlier to make certain I was agreeable to the rooms. We have a dressing room, complete with bathing area and this lovely bedchamber with sitting room over by the fireplace. I told him it was perfect."

"It is." Her eyes wanted to absorb her surroundings. Since being here last—Bridgeton, or more likely Amelia—had had the room done over, but she supposed there would be time to inspect it later. Now she wanted to change into her new night rail Miranda had bought her. Her sister-in-law promised it would have Robert tearing it from her body. Mary hoped that was a good thing.

"I will only need but a few minutes." Inside the dressing room she went over to the bowl and pitcher and washed up while she waited for Lucy. When she arrived she helped Mary undress down to her chemise, then took out all the pins from her blonde hair and brushed it until it shined. "Your hair looks lovely. Would you like my help changing into your night rail?"

"No, thank you."

"Good night, Mrs. Smythe, and may I say congratulations on your nuptials."

"Thank you."

It wasn't hard to find the gift from Miranda as it was wrapped in lovely cream tissue paper and ribbon with a note attached that read, "To Mary, may your wedding night be what dreams are made of. Love, Miranda."

She gently untied the ribbon, tore the tissue and gasped at the most beautiful, soft, and delicate sheer white night rail trimmed in light blue lace, she'd ever witnessed. Hurrying, she took off her chemise and slipped the soft fabric over her head and tied up the pale blue laces which went from the low neckline down to her naval. One glance in the looking glass and Mary gasped. Her hand covered her mouth and her eyes widened. Was that her gazing back at her? She resembled a nymph from a fairytale. A beautiful nymph. Mary knew she was pretty enough, but beautiful? Tonight she looked beautiful and her face heated at the gossamer thin linen that hid nothing from the eyes. Her nipples were rosy and hard. The triangle of dark blonde hair at the apex of her thighs could be seen.

Her brother would be aghast if he knew Miranda gave her this? It was indecent, gorgeous, and oh so pretty. For the first time in her life she felt like a woman. She picked up the tissue, looking for a matching wrapper. Nothing. Did Miranda expect her to face Robert dressed in practically nothing? Evidently. She thought about putting on her own wrapper, but it would spoil the beauty. Besides, hadn't Miranda said Robert would only rip it off her body anyway. Mary swallowed loudly. That would leave her naked. Only one way to find out. Inhaling and exhaling several times for courage, she exited the dressing room to find her husband standing in front of the hearth, stripped down to his breeches and nothing else. No stockings, boots, or shirt. A tumbler of amber liquid cradled in his hand. She looked her fill before he realized she stood behind him. She hushed her gasp when her eyes fell on what looked like whip marks crisscrossing his back and snaking up his shoulders. Several small round pucker holes, most likely from bullets or knives also marred his back—the two from recently still red and slightly swollen. After taking care of him twice after being attacked on two separate occasions she knew his job to be dangerous, but deadly? Heart pounding, her hand flew to her chest and she whimpered.

He spun around and froze, dropping his now empty glass to the carpet. "Mary."

Her cheeks engulfed in flames at the raw desire shining from his eyes making her forget about his dangerous job. It took all her self-control not to cover herself. Her body squirmed, wanting so badly to be hidden. But she stood her ground.

"Robert," Mary said breathlessly as she eyed the front of him. Who knew men's chests were so beautiful? Hard muscle everywhere. Dark hair dusted his chest and a darker more pronounced line dipped into the top of his breeches. Her throat cleared as she tried not to count the scars marring the front of his body as well. "Robert," she repeated.

Three large strides and he faced her, his eyes alight with wonder and desire. "You are beautiful. I'm not worthy of you." His eyes dimmed.

"You are. You are the only man I love or will ever love. You make me feel safe and wanted. You make me laugh and right now I feel things I don't understand, but I know you do. And you will show me how to love you with my body. My heart and soul already belong to you. Tonight my body will as well. Don't ever doubt your worth of me." Mary placed the palm of her hand on his cheek, and he leaned into it. "You are more than worthy."

His fingers toyed with the ties to her night rail. "This is the most beautiful shift I have ever seen. As lovely as you look in it, it needs to go."

Their eyes locked, her breath suspended as his large fingers unlaced the front of her night rail. Each and every time his knuckles brushed against her, Mary felt a pull down low. When at last he finished with the ties, he parted the fabric, slipped it off her shoulders and before she could inhale much needed air, it pooled down around her feet, leaving her bare. Her body shivered.

"Are you cold?" he whispered with such concern it warmed her heart. Had anyone ever been so concerned with her comfort before.

"Yes. No." Mary had no idea what she was. All thought had vacated her mind.

His hands, warm and callused, drew her close and his lips descended on hers. Gently, oh so gently, he kissed her. Mary moaned or was it him? Before she knew it he scoped her up into his arms, strolled to the huge four poster bed, and came down on top of her without ever breaking their kiss. A kiss which had intensified from one second to the next. His tongue swept inside, tangled with hers as they tasted each other. Explored each other's mouth. He broke the kiss, gasping for air, and proceeded to place barely there kisses up her neck to her ear and across the other side causing her to gasp and clutch his huge shoulders.

Every inch of Mary's skin wanted to feel every inch of his. As he kissed his way down her chest and swirled his tongue around one nipple then sucked it into his mouth, her hips rose off the bed of their own accord. He controlled her body like a puppet on a string. Little sighs and moans escaped from her throat. He repeated his attentions on her other breast as one of his hands skimmed down her side to her hip and beneath her to cup her bottom. He ground his hips against her, and she gasped at the bulge in his breeches, making her wonder how the large, hard member would fit inside her? And then she blocked it out. Robert would love her and they would fit. He lifted off her and stood beside the bed, his hand going to the packet of his breeches as he stripped them off and dropped back down and continued where he'd left off. Mary was disappointed she didn't get a good look at him, so she slid her hand down between them and ran her hand up and down his silky, thick shaft, causing Robert to groan and grind into her hand.

As Mary explored, his fingers worked between her thighs, opening her folds, twirling around her nub and then his finger invaded her body and she almost jumped off the bed.

"Easy, love. Let yourself feel. Concentrate on my fingers and what they do to your body. Don't think, feel."

Mary did what he said, her hand left his shaft, and she clutched his shoulders, her nails biting into his skin as his fingers played with her sex. Down low in her belly she felt unusual. Every time Robert's finger slid inside, her hips bucked and when he pulled out they sank. Moisture covered her down there, and she didn't have the time to wonder why as he moved farther down her body. His lips placed hot, wet kisses all along her stomach and her hips. Before she knew what was happening he spread her thighs and his mouth descended there. Moans escaped her lips as he swirled his tongue, sucked and tugged on her nub, making her mind scream for more. More of the elusive tingling and feelings she didn't understand, but craved. "Robert," Mary moaned as he inserted his finger inside her over and over until she screamed, her hips thrust up, her body trembled and her mind was overcome with understanding these new and wondrous sensations.

Robert moved up her body murmuring, "Beautiful, not worthy, so precious." His mouth took her in a hard, desperate kiss as his member pushed against her, one, two, three thrusts and she tore her mouth from his and cried out in pain and he froze.

"I'm sorry. So sorry. The pain should ease," Robert groaned into her ear.

Shocked from the quick, but stabbing pain, Mary reassured her husband. "It's lessening already."

His hips moved again, slow and steady at first and the pain did indeed ease. His hand dropped between their bodies, he touched her causing her to gasp and her hips rose up to meet his. Over and over Mary tried to keep with his rhythm as her body reached for that elusive something once again. Faster, Robert thrust fast and deep, his hand caressed her womanhood over and over. Her insides throbbed around his cock, she grabbed his buttocks pulling him tighter against her as she needed...wanted...needed. She screamed as her body exploded at the same time Robert bowed up tight, growled and collapsed down onto her as warmth flooded her insides and her eyes saw millions of vibrant shooting stars.

Her entire body relaxed. Exhausted, she curled up against Robert, letting her eyelids flutter closed. "I love you," left her lips as sleep pulled her into its comforted arms.

"AND I LOVE YOU." Robert spoke the words knowing she

never heard him as she'd fallen asleep. Her body relaxed against his, her breathing evened out, and little sounds almost resembling snoring came from her luscious lips. He hugged her closer. His little, proper wife snored. It was adorable, she would be appalled.

Never, ever had he experienced anything like what just happened. Their bodies fit perfectly, and when joined together he'd finally found out what being whole meant. Being with Mary made him complete. Solidified his body, mind, and soul. Not to mention what it did to his heart. His heart wanted to explode from his chest and join with hers. Two hearts beating and existing as one. He didn't know what he'd done to deserve her, but he would spend the rest of his life worshiping and cherishing her. She was all that was pure and goodness. Freely giving her love to him, humbling him, and he would do anything to keep her happy and content.

His mind wandered to the conversation he'd had with both Bridgeton and Spencer about finances. He'd never let on that he'd invested his money wisely. Outrageous amounts of money paid to him for his private services making him perfectly capable of keeping Mary and any children they were blessed with comfortable. For a time now he'd been thinking about leaving the runners and going private. The hours he worked at his office and out on the streets of London would take him away from Mary from sunup and some days well past sundown. If he had the ability to pick his clients and the work he took on, he would be able to spend time with his wife. Time he wanted, needed, to be with her. Also, she'd never said the words, but he knew she worried about him. The scars on his body were testament to the dangers of his job. The last thing he wanted to do was cause his wife undo worry. As a private investigator he could choose not to take the dangerous assignments, leaving Mary to go about her day without worrying for his safety. As his mind spun with plans to undertake this adventure, it took over an hour to force his mind to shut down and he finally joined his wife in slumber.

Breakfast the following morning surprised Robert. All who attended their wedding sat around the large table in the formal dining room as the breakfast room wouldn't accommodate everyone. They laughed and carried on animated conversations making his heart sore. Once again he wondered what he'd ever done to get so fortunate to marry into such a loving and happy family. Even though some at the table were not related by blood, they were a family through and through to the core. For someone, such as himself, who'd never had a family, it had his throat clogged with emotions, and he actually fought back tears in his eyes. It wouldn't do to cry like a baby in front of Mary's family.

But the love he witnessed firsthand was foreign to him, and he prayed he could live up to these people's expectations. The very first time Wentworth hired him after the duchess was kidnapped, they'd sucked him into their fold. A single tear escaped down his cheek, and he used his cloth napkin to swipe it away, pretending he was wiping food off his face. Damn, but his heart was open and raw.

After Mary and Robert said their goodbyes, they traveled in a luxurious coach and four Spencer and Miranda gifted them for their wedding. Once again he fought not to embarrass himself by crying. The second, smaller vehicle that carried Mary's maid and her trunks, Spencer let them borrow. Robert's belongings filled but half a trunk. Besides the two drivers, they were escorted by two outriders and a groom. And, of course, Robert had enough weapons inside the carriage to hold off an army. He wasn't about to take any chances after what happened the last time they took to the roads. The road to Sussex should go smoothly and not take very long.

Robert could barely wait to spend a fortnight in the

country worshiping his new bride, who snuggled next to him fighting to stay awake. "Sleep my love. You deserve rest after last night."

Her head rose up off his shoulder and she smiled shyly, her cheeks a nice becoming shade of pink. "I never dreamt it would be...so amazing."

His hand ran over her hair and gently pressed her head back to his shoulder. "It was. But rest now because when we arrive in Sussex I may keep you up all night with my undivided attention worshiping your body."

Mary's chest rose and fell against his side. "I would like that." She paused and when she spoke again her voice came to his ears soft and hesitant. "Is there a way for me to worship your body?"

Instant tightness in his buckskin breeches had him groaning. "Yes. Would you like me to teach you?"

"Yes, thank you."

Thank you? She thanked him because he would teach her how to pleasure his body. How had he ever gotten so lucky.

At the first sight of The Rose Cottage, Robert swallowed. They'd said a small estate. If that rose colored, brick monstrosity, beautiful as it glowed in the sunset, was small, what did a medium or large estate resemble. And this belonged to his wife? He really did not deserve her.

"Oh, I haven't been here since I was a young girl, but I always loved this cottage of Grandmother's. With the rose and white brick, it always reminded me of a doll house. Not in size, of course, but in its feminine lines. I never imagined she would gift it to me for a wedding present. Gift it to us."

"No, you said it right the first time. It is yours and will go to our children. If anything happens to me, I want you to have a home of your own. The house in London is rented and not ours. Although we could purchase or build one if you would like?"

She sat forward and looked questioning at him. "Build? Where on earth would we get such money? I know my dowry is large, but five thousand pounds only goes so far."

"I made good investments in the past. We have plenty of money, even without yours. I would prefer if we didn't touch a shilling of yours and kept it for our children."

Mary's face lit up, and her lips spread into a wide smile. "You, my husband, are full of surprises. I do love surprises. Does my brother know?"

"Yes." No sooner were the words out of his mouth when the groomsman opened the door, let down the stairs, and Robert exited the coach, turning back to help his bride down. Tucking her arm around his they pivoted around and came face to face with the staff.

"Oh, dear," Mary said. "I don't know their names. It's been ages since I've been here. I should have asked Grandmother."

A small, middle-aged man stepped forward and bowed. Welcome home, Mr. and Mrs. Smythe. I'm Harrison, your butler. May I present the staff?"

Mary nudged his side. They were waiting for him. "Thank you for the welcome, Harrison. And yes, please make the introductions."

Mary whispered into his ear. "Well done."

Introductions complete, the housekeeper and butler's wife, Harriot, led them to their chambers. Two large bedrooms, one masculine done in navy and burgundy, one done in shades of pink and cream and very feminine. Each having a dressing room and sitting area with a connecting door. More room than they needed. And one extra bed. Robert planned on spending every night in the same bed as his wife. His insides tightened. Did Mary want her own bed? Only one way to find out. After the housekeeper left them he said, "I hope you will sleep with me at night and not in your bed alone." His heart constricted, and he held his breath awaiting Mary's reply.

"I will be sleeping where you are."

His lungs and heart easing, Robert approached her, wrapped his arms around her waist, and swung her around until they were both dizzy and breathless, and then he kissed her with all his love and desire.

CHAPTER TWELVE

PLACING HER HAND ON HER STOMACH, WHICH ROLLED IN silent protest from the rich food she'd consumed at dinner, made Elizabeth wonder what was happening to her. The past two weeks her stomach had been sensitive from morning to night. She fought queasiness as Sophie, her ladies' maid, dressed up her hair for that evening's masquerade ball held at the Earl and Countess of Edgewater's London residence.

Tonight's ball didn't have a theme, which disappointed her. She loved dressing up and taking on the costume's persona. Tonight all she'd wear would be a mask. A beautiful violet mask to complement the trim on her light pink gown. Sequins and feathers decorated the mask that covered her face from her top lip up to her forehead and beyond with the feathers.

She didn't understand why they traveled with their masks on, but Spencer explained there would be a crush of carriages as they neared the earl's residence. Midnight would be the unveiling. Inside the coach, Spencer and Miranda sat facing forward and Elizabeth faced backward. Grandmother and Mother had stayed in the country after Mary and Robert's wedding. Sighing, she closed her eyes and pictured the love radiating from Mary and Robert's eyes during the ceremony and during the wedding breakfast.

Her stomach rolled. Did Edward look at her like that? Why was she questioning his love? Because they had been back from the country for a sennight and he'd yet to propose. They had agreed to wait until after Mary and Robert's nuptials. They were done. What was keeping him? Elizabeth knew he'd asked her brother for permission and was granted it. Had he changed his mind and didn't want to marry her anymore? How would she explain to the man she eventually took as a husband as to why she wasn't a virgin? And then it hit her, hard and sudden as though she'd been wacked off the side of the head with a board. Could she be with child? The symptoms were there. Sickness, sensitive breasts, and having to relieve herself more than usual. Cramps as though her courses were coming but didn't. Which, now that she thought about it, were overdo by, she counted in her head, ten days. She gasped and covered her mouth, eyes wide with fear.

Two sets of eyes focused on her. "Are you ill Elizabeth?" Miranda asked.

Gulping air, she hoped to be able to answer. If Amesbury didn't marry her now with a special license what would happen to her? She'd be ruined and her baby scorned for life. She could deal with be ruined but not forcing her child to a life of misery and scorn from being born a bastard. Tears leaked out but fortunately were absorbed by the mask. "I'm well. I was just thinking of something I forgot to do."

"You made quite a noise. Most unladylike as well," Spencer teased. "Indeed, if you are unwell we can turn around and bring you home. Miranda and I don't mind arriving more than fashionably late. Especially as no one will know who we are. I will extend apologies to Amesbury for your absence."

Part of her wanted to run home, bury herself beneath her coverlet and cry herself to sleep. The other part wanted to see Edward. Tell him about the baby. Well, at least explain her worry about a baby, since nothing had been confirmed. "No. I'm looking forward to tonight. I love masquerade balls. Besides I hope to nudge Edward along with his proposal. I can't think what he is waiting for."

Clearing his throat, her brother looked at her through his plain black mask. "You know he will propose. Give him time. It's not every day a man gives up his freedom and attaches himself to a ball and chain."

"Funny, brother. Funny. Will this crush of carriages ever end?" Just then their door opened and the stairs lowered. "Good. I thought we'd never get out of this confined vehicle." Her lungs needed air to hopefully settle the abundance of nerves that had taken over her body."

Spencer held his hand out, first he helped his wife down then his sister. And then she found herself in a crush of people she didn't recognize. She couldn't even see Spencer or Miranda anymore. Indeed, she may as well walk around trying to ascertain who was who and find Edward. She stopped on one side of the dance floor, her eyes scanning the room for the man who held her heart when a tall gentleman approached. Why had she believed she liked masquerade balls? Gentlemen she didn't know, or did she, could walk up to her and converse. Rules of etiquette were stretched thin on a night such as this.

"Good evening." He bowed.

Not enough words spoken for her to recognize the voice. Although she did know the voice didn't belong to anyone she knew well. "Good evening to you as well." She dropped a curtsy.

"Would you care to dance?" Dark eyes, penetrating through wide holes of a full-face mask in black, ran blatantly up and down her body, eyes not the color of Edward's. No. She didn't like masquerades anymore. How could this man look at her as though he wanted to eat her up? Act as if they were familiar with each other. There was nothing about him to think they'd ever met. Which brought to mind, could one be rude while hidden behind a mask and refuse an offer to dance? Although, something appeared familiar about his eyes.

"I can read the look in your eyes." He held out his gloved hand. "It is just a dance. I promise not to ravish you on the floor in plain sight of all the attendees. I believe the mask is making you uneasy. I promise I'm not a libertine but a gentleman inside and out."

Elizabeth's mouth opened to scold him for his shocking words, but nothing but a silent, "Oh," exited. Before the shock left her, he'd placed her hand on his forearm and led her onto the crowded dance floor. Figured a waltz would play, and she found herself held far too close. Society rules were broken on the dance floor as well tonight. Her eyes moved around from couple to couple. Was there anyone adhering to etiquette or society rules attending? How could Spencer have left her alone to her own devices once they arrived? Left her in a cage, locked with a lion ready to devour her. Trembles took over each and every nerve in her body, making it difficult to keep up with the steps.

"Relax, I promise not to bite you or ravish you, whatever it is your mind is conjuring up." He exhaled. "I thought perhaps you could find your Lord Amesbury from the dance floor." His full lips turned up into a crooked grin baring somewhat straight white teeth. "I presume that is what you were doing standing on the side, your head pivoting back and forth until I thought it would roll off your shoulders."

"Do I know you?" Chills ran up and down her spine, radiating out from where his hand splayed against the small of her back. "Please remove your hand from my back and put it where it belongs."

Another grin and his black eyes twinkled. "Apologies, my dear." Leisurely he moved his hand to her waist. "I seldom dance—I'd forgotten where to place my hand."

"Rubbish." Elizabeth wasn't one to be intimidated, but he'd managed it the moment he'd approached her, but no more. She wouldn't cower like an innocent debutant. Which of course, she wasn't. There was a time when she used to shock people with what she said. He was playing games with her, like she used to do. "I believe you knew exactly what you were doing...ah...Mr....My Lord...heaven forbid...Your Grace."

Leaning down he whispered into her ear and she fought the urge to move away. "I can be whomever your heart desires."

"Stop it. I refuse to play your games. Since you obviously know who I am, I deserve the courtesy of knowing who you are."

A deep chuckle answered her. "Look around my dear. People love to be incognito. I'm no different. It is not my fault I recognized you when you arrived."

"Is there a reason you sought me out?" She may as well come right out and ask him. If he could be rude and play games so could she.

"As a matter of fact there is. For two completely different reasons." He paused, probably for suspense. "A Lady Penelope Seabrook. Although Lady is a bit of a stretch considering her origins."

Elizabeth glared at him and growled. Yes, growled. "Don't you dare disrespect her."

The stranger nodded his head. "Apologies. I meant no disrespect, just stating the facts as I see them. Please tell me she is attending this evening?"

He surprised her. What on earth did he want with Pene-

lope? Elizabeth hadn't seen the duke and duchess or Penelope, although she'd heard they would be in attendance. "I
heard she would be attending with her brother, the duke and
his duchess, but I haven't seen them. What, pray tell do you
want with Lady Penelope?"

The man had the audacity to laugh, deep and throaty.
"That is none of your concern, my dear sweet lady. Next ques-
tion. If I'm not mistaken your sister is married to a Mr.
Smythe."

Elizabeth's head snapped up and looked directly into his
dark eyes. "Who are you and what do you want with my
brother-in-law? Are you trying to cause trouble for them?"

"Easy, Miss Spencer." He looked around. "Keep your voice
down. I may have a job for him. He's been hired by your
brother before, as well at Wentworth and Northborough. I'm
trying to ascertain how loyal and trustworthy he is."

"Loyal." Lowering her voice, and ignoring the prickles up
her spine, she leaned closer to this stranger. "There is no
more loyal gentleman in all of England. Loyal to the Crown
and his clients. Which makes me wonder why you sought me
out. Why not speak to my brother, the duke, or the earl?"

"Bloody hell," he said, and for the first time he sounded
exasperated. "Can't recognize any of them. You were the first
person I identified."

"I'm still confused as to why you noticed me. I don't know
you. Nothing about you is familiar."

"Ah, saved by the orchestra, my dear. May I escort you
back to your corner of the ballroom? Actually," he grinned, "I
see your marquess. I'll delivery you to him."

At the corner of the ballroom, the stranger bowed. "You
will find him in the dark amongst the potted palms and
pillars. Where couples go for liaisons." Was that pity she
glimpsed in his dark eyes?

Chills once again climbed up her spine. What on earth

would Edward be doing lurking in the shadows. Where couples, married and unmarried, went to steal kisses or more. Now her stomach churned and she swallowed, trying to keep her supper down. Standing on the edge of the dimly lit area, she squinted into the dark, listening to the murmuring voices, hoping to recognize Edward's.

A lady's voice giggling caught her attention, then her sickly sweet voice spoke. "Come now Lord A., we miss you at the Red Poppy. It's been an age since you graced us with your presence. I miss our trysts. We can duck into one of the rooms off this hall, and I'll toss up my skirts like I used to. Remember how you loved to fuck me, feast on me."

Elizabeth's hand covered her mouth to keep from screaming. There was no mistaking who Lord A. was, even if he'd yet to speak.

"Lady S., perhaps another time."

Oh God, it was Edward, even though she didn't want to believe it. Her knees buckled and she grabbed a column to keep from collapsing in a heap on the floor. Air vacated her lungs, she thought she might die as her heart shattered into a thousand pieces.

"May I assist you, Miss Spencer?"

The large stranger, without waiting for Elizabeth to reply, curled his arm around hers and led her into the ballroom and directly toward her brother and Miranda.

"I finally recognized someone, besides you." Several feet from Spencer, the stranger removed his arm and bowed. "I'm sorry for what you witnessed." With that he disappeared into the crowd.

Elizabeth continued the few steps to her brother and Miranda's side. "I'm sorry. I'm feeling unwell. I'll take the carriage and send it back."

"Nonsense," Miranda said as she glanced at Spencer, looking worried. "We will all go."

It seemed the longest carriage ride Elizabeth had ever endured. She ripped off her mask as soon as she sat against the squabs and fought harder than she ever had not to break down and cry. Finally, they arrived home. She said a quick goodnight to Spencer and Miranda and hurried up the staircase, down the hall to her room. Sophie was waiting for her and helped her get ready for bed in her dressing room. When her pantaloons were removed they were stained.

"You have your courses. Let me get you the strips of cloth."

Dismissing her maid, once she was settled for bed, Elizabeth climbed beneath the covers, her hand on her belly, and great sobs racked her body. Crying from relief of not being with child and crying because she wasn't pregnant. Dear God, she was a mess. And after what she'd heard tonight, and knowing she wasn't increasing, she could break off whatever it was she had with Edward.

It was obvious from his actions tonight, he didn't want to marry her. Or if he did, he would not be faithful to her, which she could not abide. And what sort of place was the Red Poppy? She'd never heard of such an establishment. Perhaps it was a house of ill repute, and the lady tonight was a courtesan. Perhaps she was Edward's mistress. Did it matter? No. Elizabeth's heart had split open and withered to nothingness at the ball. Edward no longer meant anything to her. In fact, she would never love, trust, or give herself to another. Spinsterhood wouldn't be so bad. Her loving family would be enough. Their love would sustain her until she took her last breath. She would be the best aunt to Mary and Robert's children. Miranda and Spencer's as well if they were blessed with a family. She'd never need a babe of her own. Perhaps she could live with Mary at The Rose Cottage.

Turning onto her side, curled up tight, tears streaming down her face staining her pillow, she fought not to hear the woman's voice. Thank God she couldn't see them clearly, only their outlines. Because if she had, she didn't know what she might have done. It was better this way. If she had to tell herself that every day for the rest of her life so be it. Being married to a man who could not be faithful and probably didn't love her would not do. She deserved better even if she didn't want it anymore.

"WHY WON'T SHE SEE ME?" Edward collapsed into a chair opposite Spencer's desk and took the offered glass of brandy, wasting no time in tossing back the entire contents. The burn sliding down his throat and settling in his belly was a welcome relief. He appreciated the respite from feeling as though the entire world was out of control and playing tricks on him. He'd finally managed to get his life right-side up and suddenly it was upside down again.

"Did you two argue last night?" Elizabeth's brother eyed him over the rim of his glass.

"No. I never even saw her. Did she attend?"

"Yes."

His insides churned. How could he not have seen her? Why hadn't she approached him? Damn last night. It hadn't gone well. The moment he'd stepped inside Lord and Lady Edgewater's townhome he'd recognized several questionable members of the *ton* from his opium days. "I never saw her nor you and Miranda."

"I assure you, the three of us were in attendance. Although we didn't stay more than an hour. We were separated from Elizabeth soon after our arrival. I saw her dance with a tall gentleman I didn't recognize. Not long after, she said she felt unwell and wished to leave."

Anger coiled up tight inside Amesbury's chest. "Who was

the man? What did he say to her? Did he behave shockingly toward her? Overly familiar?" During a masquerade anything was possible. Strange how he once enjoyed hiding behind the mask.

Inhaling and exhaling, Spencer sipped his brandy. "I honestly can't say." Placing his glass on his desk, he sat back and crossed his arms on his chest. "I admit it wasn't long after the dance that she came to us begging to leave. She did appear upset, but you know women, they are hard to read and she didn't offer any explanation."

"Damn it." Amesbury jumped up and paced the small office. "If I never saw her last night, and before that things were good between us, then what the devil happened?"

Time went by. Spencer stared at him with intense blue eyes the same hue at Elizabeth's.

"What?" Amesbury barked.

"I always wondered about the time you had that mysteries illness and your betrothal to Lady Beth was broken. Rumors ran rampart as to the reason. Pray tell me, does my sister know?"

Amesbury sputtered, "About my illness or the broken betrothal?"

"Both."

Collapsing back onto the seat he held up his empty glass. "I need more." After it was replenished he downed half of it. He'd save the rest until he spilled his guts. "The only two people who know what mysterious illness I had is Wentworth and Myles if you don't count my trusted housekeeper, valet, butler, and family physician." He paused and inhaled for courage. "Ever since the carriage accident that took the lives of my parents and sister, I'd been addicted to laudanum. Years of hiding my drug addiction proved successful. Trying to get off the vile stuff not so. I took the drug in part for the pain I experience in my back and legs on a daily basis. I hide my injury well. Even you have never seen me use a cane. But I assure you, once I'm in the privacy of my home I use it faithfully. If there is ever a day the pain is too intense to go without the cane, I stay home in solitude. I will not have anyone think me weak or a cripple."

"Christ, how the hell have you hidden this? It's been years." Spencer bellowed.

"I had help from Wentworth and Myles when it came to not having aid of a cane. They did not know about the misuse of laudanum. But not long after those two returned from America, and while I was betrothed to Lady Beth, I took too much opium and almost died. Truthfully I wanted to die. My butler sent word to my friends, who were shocked to find out what had been going on, and they spent days, weeks helping me through my withdrawals—tying me down in bed so I couldn't hurt myself. And many other things too embarrassing to speak of. I've not touched a drop of the stuff since. I promise you I am worthy, at least I think I'm worthy, of your sister. I love her and would do anything to make her happy."

A lengthy pause had Edward's blood pumping loudly inside his ears. "Bloody hell Spencer, say something, anything."

"I'm processing it all and trying to remember back to that time. I was trying to win Bella's heart away from Myles. But one would have had to be an idiot not to have heard the rumors surrounding you. However, your use of opium never once was whispered through the drawing rooms of London. How did you hide it? Someone other than Wentworth and Myles had to have known."

"Yes, well, there are people who know. Others who partake in the drug. Others who visit opium dens such as I had. But they would never talk. We sign a code of silence."

"A...what..." Spencer choked out.

He found himself chuckling. Couldn't help it. It did sound ridiculous. "Well, even opium eaters have a code of ethics."

"What else do I need to know?"

"Nothing, unless you want to know about my betrothal. And by the way, Elizabeth already knows about this." At Spencer's nod, Edward sighed. "After the night I...over indulged, Wentworth paid a visit to Lady Beth's father and begged off on my behalf. I don't know what he said or how he did it, but that is all I know. And I owe the duke my eternal gratitude for it."

"Last night." Finishing his drink and placing his empty glass on the desk, Spencer eyed him. "Tell me everything that happened last night from the moment you entered the ball."

Edward leaned back in the chair and rested one ankle on top of the other knee. "Shit. There were several acquaintances I recognized from the den I used to visit. The Red Poppy." His heart lodged up into his throat, making it difficult to continue. He rubbed his chest, hoping his heart went back into place. "There was a time when I walked around looking for Elizabeth. I couldn't find her in the ballroom so I ventured out into the hallways. Dark and private. Why I thought she might be there I have no idea. A woman approached. She recognized me immediately. She called me Lord A." His eyes closed and he fought the guilt and disgust trying to swallow him into the dark abyss. "She mentioned how we used to, excuse me if I use her crude language, fuck. How she used to toss up her skirts for me."

His head dropped into his hands and he groaned. "I knew I would not be able to keep my past secret forever. I told Elizabeth everything, except about the opium. Bloody hell, I still haven't discussed my need for a cane either. But I planned on confessing all before I asked for her hand. Owing it to her to know all about my degenerate and disgusting past. Sex with strangers, orgies. I'd wake up in the morning and have no recollection of my previous night's behavior." He raised his head and stared right into Spencer's hard eyes. "I promise you that is all in the past. I'm not that person anymore. Haven't been in a long time. You never have to worry about your sister after we marry."

"Is there a possibility she overheard this conversation with the...woman...in the alcove?"

Before Edward could answer, the door burst open and in fell Elizabeth, wide-eyed, resembling a warrior princess ready to do battle and protect all at once.

"Will you please excuse us brother," she uttered through gritted teeth.

Spencer's eyes moved from Edward to Elizabeth. "My dear sister, you appear distraught. Do I need to stay and protect Amesbury?"

Her beautiful, wild eyes pierced Spencer. If they could spur forth shards of glass her brother would be gravely injured. "If he cannot protect himself then he is not worth of my time or your efforts in doing so."

"Then," he bowed, "I will leave you. However, before I do, might I remind you of my collection of priceless paper weights on the shelf. They would do significant damage to the plaster and windows."

"Remove yourself, brother."

CHAPTER THIRTEEN

BREATHE. ELIZABETH COULD HARDLY TAKE IN AIR AS HER insides, including her lungs, constricted up tightly. Her heart and mind fought for the right to tell her what to do and feel. Her heart cracked wide open at what Edward had endured. However, her mind had a brain of its own, wanting to be furious with him for keeping all that had happened to him from her. Oh, she was furious, but at him or the circumstances she couldn't be sure. He'd hinted at doing unspeakable things, but she hadn't imagined anything such as he had. In fact, Elizabeth had all but forgotten—with all the excitement of Mary's wedding and her confidence Edward and she would marry next—about the things he'd hinted at doing but kept avoiding telling her.

Well, now she understood. How would he have broached the subject. *"I've lived the life of a degenerate. There was a time in my life I had no morals whatsoever. I participated in orgies, had sex with strangers."* Dear God, how did one get over this. Her hand clutched her chest, and her weak knees almost sent her crashing to the floor. The war engaging inside her mind and heart reached a crescendo and a humming so loud she thought she might cast up her accounts. *Breathe. Inhale. Exhale. Slow and steady.* She could do this. She needed to do this.

"Amesbury." Before she knew what their future beheld, she would not use his Christian name. God, how that stung. Forcing her legs onward, she took her place at Spencer's vacated chair and somehow managed to look Amesbury in the eye. "First, I must apologize for listening at the door. It wasn't my intention. Truthfully, I didn't know you were still here after I refused to see you. I came to speak with my brother in private." Elizabeth paused, cleared her throat hoping the lump lodged there would vanish. "When I heard your raised voice, I could hardly leave. What happened to you and what you lived through weighs heavily on my heart and mind. I'm going to need time to come to terms with the gentleman I know and the gentleman you hid from me."

"I..."

A quivering hand came up, halting his words. "I can't have this conversation with you today. Please just let me say my peace."

His eyes closed, he inhaled and exhaled loudly, and his eyes popped open. The uncertainty, embarrassment, and pain she witnessed in the depths of his hazel eyes tugged on her heart strings. Elizabeth pushed it aside for now, knowing the look would haunt her dreams for many nights to come. "Last night when I found you in the darkness meant for liaisons and I heard that woman speak, I almost vomited at the words she used. For surely she couldn't be speaking about my Edw... Amesbury. She had intimate knowledge of you, which I know many women do. It was how she said it. How she treated you. I never imagined places like these existed, never mind members of the *ton* visited them. I gather from the woman that the Red Poppy is a place where one goes to get opium, do whatever one does with the drug, and have sex. A den of iniquity. A place where people go to lose themselves in opium and wickedness of the flesh."

"Please..."

The pleading in his voice once again tugged at her, but she would not allow it. She would be strong. Before she could commit to a future with him, she needed to know his past indiscretions wouldn't plague their marriage. The last thing she would allow and had to be certain would never happen was for his past to haunt their marriage. For if it did, they would end up hating each other and being miserable. Something she would not allow. Most of her friends and family married for love and were happy. She needed, wanted that. Until last night, she knew they would have that. Now...only time would tell. Time for her to come to terms with this part of him she hadn't known. A part that disgusted her. Perhaps Elizabeth was too innocent and naive. If they'd already been married or affianced, the point would be moot. Dealing with it would not be an option. She would have to get past it. She wished she could go back to yesterday and make it all go away.

Abruptly standing, nearly knocking the chair to the ground, Elizabeth mumbled, "I must go. Please excuse me." As fast as her legs could move, she ran from the room, her skirts hiked up almost to her knees. She ran down the hall, up the stairs, and into her chambers diving facedown onto her bed.

With a soft knock on the door, Miranda's voice called out, "Elizabeth, may I come in?"

Rolling over and skootching up so her back rested against the headboard, using pillows to cushion her back and head from the wood, she answered, "Yes."

Her sister-in-law looked worried as she made her way toward the bed and sat down on the edge. "Spencer told me what happened."

Shame burned her cheeks. "I'm shocked and embarrassed and mortified that you know," she cried. "That my brother knows. I don't think I'll be able to look Wentworth or Myles in the eye ever again. They knew what sort of man Amesbury was and yet..."

"Yes, they knew," Miranda interjected, "and yet, they are still considered the very closest of friends. They obviously don't dwell on the man's regrettable past. His mistakes and transgressions."

"Easy for them. They are men and the world is different for them. Besides, they were not planning on marrying him or in love with him."

"No. Of course not. How they reacted and how you reacted are vastly different." Miranda paused, shimmied up the bed, sitting beside her and wrapping an arm around her shoulders. The touch soothed Elizabeth's frayed nerves. "I'm quite convinced Amesbury would be appalled if he knew I knew his secrets. But your brother and I share everything. Not to mention, how could he explain the rift between you two. I would not stop asking questions as to why you and Amesbury were not together anymore."

Numb, the pain bombarding her since last evening turned numb, giving Elizabeth some respite from the physical ache. The mental anguish still forged on, no end in sight. "I want to go back a day. I want to be ignorant of his past. I wish to forget everything from last night and this day. I want to love him again. Things transpired between us." Elizabeth took a deep breath for courage. "I'm no longer a virgin. If I don't marry him, who will have me?"

"Oh, my dear sweet girl." Miranda hugged her closer. "That is not true. If you cannot forgive or move forward with Amesbury, there will be another gentleman to love you and for you to love. But first you need to be absolutely positive you are not with child."

Disgusted with herself for crying, Elizabeth swiped away the tears clinging to her cheeks. "I first thought I might be, but my courses came last night."

A deep sigh came from Miranda. "Good. Now back to what I was saying, you know what happened to me with Henry Baker, Aunt Violet's husband. How he raped me?"

Hearing the words rape twisted up Elizabeth's insides. So much for believing her numb. "Yes."

"Your brother loves me and married me regardless. Oh, some snobbish, boorish gentleman would believe me ruined and not worth the ground beneath his boots, but not Spencer. Of course, it didn't hurt that we had a past together, but still. If and when you decide to move forward, do not believe for one moment, you are ruined for love or marriage. Men do not come to the marriage bed chaste. Anyone worthy of your love will understand. There is so much to think about and decide, don't let your lack of virginity come into play."

"Thank you," Elizabeth said around the tears clogging her throat.

"For what?"

"For making me feel better. At least a little better. I still have the whole opium and potential sex scandal to contend with. Can you imagine if the gossip sheets got wind of Amesbury's past shocking behavior? My God, he'd be ruined and when he marries, his wife would be ruined as well."

"Yes, he would...they would. It won't happen. He's kept it secret for this long."

"Yes, but what if it did get out?" Poor Amesbury, it would likely kill him. See, there was hope. She still had feelings for him. Feelings of pity anyway.

"What are you thinking?" her sister-in-law asked.

"That I have feelings of pity for Amesbury at the very least. It's not as though I can vanquish my feelings and love for him in a day. They may be strained to the breaking point, but I can't dissolve them instantly. What I need to figure out is if I can live with his past. Because if it haunts me or I don't trust him, then our relationship is doomed. I need a man who is faithful, and loves me beyond reason." Elizabeth scoffed. "Loves me a little at least." Silent tears came back to slip down her face. "I'm so confused Miranda. I don't know what to do? I've always prided myself on knowing my mind. Of going after what I want, even if I exasperated my brother and grandmother in the process. Mother doesn't count as she never took any interest in our lives. I keep thinking what if Grandmother knew? How shocked would she be? Would she demand I never see Amesbury ever again? That he never grace the rooms of our home again?" Thoughts fought for purchase inside Elizabeth's brain.

Forgive him. Don't forgive him.

He loves me. I love him.

He can't be trusted. Trust him.

Can I allow him to touch me after knowing he'd had sex and orgies with women, possibly men?

He needs me. I need him. I don't need him.

His hands are soiled. His body tainted.

"Miranda," Elizabeth cried out as she buried her face in her hands and sobbed. "I can't...I don't...I'm confused."

Miranda's warm hand rubbed her back in gentle circles. "Easy now, try to ease your mind. I know it is hard. You are a highly intelligent woman, brave and strong. When you least expect it, your answers will come. Why don't you lie down, and I will stay with you until you fall asleep? Perhaps a nap will ease all your concerns and nagging thoughts. Mayhap when you awaken and are refreshed, you will be able to look more objectively on the situation. Right now you are in shock and highly emotional, as to be expected. Take a nap and then a step back and things should be clearer. I pray they are clearer for both your sakes."

Elizabeth slid beneath the coverlet, snuggled up to Miranda's warm side, and willed herself to sleep. All she had to do was shut down her mind, stitch her heart together, inflate her lungs and then perhaps, she could drop into dreamland. Dream of Edward as she knew him when she had visited his country estate.

EDWARD SAT STRAIGHT and stiff in Wentworth's study with his other good friend Myles. Both listened to him rant and rave for a quarter of an hour with pity on their faces. Pity—Edward didn't like pity. He hated anyone pitying him. He'd caused his problems, he didn't need sympathy, only help in winning Elizabeth's heart back. Now that she knew the truth about his past, he had nothing else to hide from her. She knew it all. He only wished he'd had the chance to explain himself. Not to mention the new problem which arose an hour ago.

"Tell us about the blackmailer's threat?" Wentworth said as he splashed brandy into three glasses and handed them out.

"Just that they require ten thousand pounds to keep quiet. Obviously it is someone who frequented the Red Poppy. My guess is Lady Silverton. She didn't take my rejection of her advances at the masquerade ball well. Also, word has it her husband has squandered their fortune on his mistresses and numerous by-blows."

"Has anyone, besides Lady Silverton, approached you since your Red Poppy days?" Myles asked as he lit a cheroot and took a deep inhale.

"No. Never. I should've known secrets never remain hidden forever. Not when one is titled and wealthy. My first instinct is to pay the damn money. I can well afford it. My second thought is if I do, it will never end. I'll live in fear of exposure. Day in and day out I'll be looking over my shoulder for the blackmailer to pounce. I'll never be able to marry Elizabeth and live peacefully. My past will always follow me...haunt me."

"Perhaps not." Wentworth leaned forward in his chair behind his desk, opposite him. "You can hire Smythe. He should be back from his honeymoon any day now."

Fingers stabbed through his hair. "Dash it all, just what I need is Mary finding out. I know about client privileges, but this is Elizabeth's brother-in-law and sister. I'll never be able to show my face in Spencer's house again."

"Don't be so hard on yourself," the duke said. "We have all done things we regret. Things we hope never see the light of day. Become public knowledge or printed in the gossip rags."

"Indeed, but I almost wish it would come out and ruin me and be over with." Edward ignored the gasps from the other occupants of the room. "I could then move to my country estate and rusticate for the rest of my life." He paused and then forged on. "Hopefully with Elizabeth as my bride by my side. If not, then I'm fine with living my life alone. It's probably no less than I deserve."

"The devil you say," Myles scoffed. "You deserve more than rusticating in the country for life. Unless it is what you prefer. Is it?"

"In some ways it is. I wouldn't be looking over my shoulder for someone to stab me in the back and laugh about it. However, after I leave here I plan on visiting Lady Silverton and threatening her with exposure. Two can play at this game. I expect my problem to end with this visit. She would be ruined far more than me if our visits to the Red Poppy became public knowledge."

"Capital idea," Myles said. "Back to Elizabeth. There must be something you are not telling us. Anything that would force Spencer to insist on a marriage between the two of you?" Myles always did love a good scandal, as long as it didn't involve him or his family or friends.

If Edward told Spencer the truth, he would make Elizabeth marry him. Could he do that to her? Force her against her wishes? Most likely she would hate him for the rest of their married lives. "Yes. And don't repeat a word of this. I bedded her."

"Spencer doesn't suspect?" Wentworth asked.

"If he does, he didn't say anything. Or perhaps he asked and I denied it. Hell, I can't recall half the conversation. And when Elizabeth interrupted us, I fumbled with words and could hear nothing but buzzing inside my brain. You should have seen her."

Wentworth raised his brows. "I can imagine. I saw something similar on Emma's face when she believed I won her father's fortune *and her* in a card game."

"Indeed I remember. Myles and I were in the room at the time. And yes, the expressions were similar if I recall the look on your Emma's face. Can I risk Elizabeth's wrath and hatred if I confess to Spencer?"

Wentworth poured two fingers in each glass of his expensive brandy. "Tell Spencer and marry the woman you love. Deal with her anger after the vows have been spoken. I thank God every day I was able to convince Emma not to leave our marriage and flee to America. Marry Elizabeth and do all you can to earn her forgiveness. If you don't marry her now she may be lost to you forever."

CHAPTER FOURTEEN

"HE WHAT...YOU WHAT?" ELIZABETH SHRIEKED AS BLIND furry overtook her.

Spencer motioned to the vacant chair facing his desk. "Sit before you collapse. You have that look about you."

Elizabeth huffed as she begrudgingly took a seat, back stiff and she glared at her brother. "How could you decide my future for me?"

Her brother sat forward in his chair and poured a splash of brandy and slid it toward his sister. "Take a sip and relax."

"I've never taken spirits."

"I know that. But sip it anyway. You look shocked and ready to kill someone. And I'd rather that someone not be me."

"Fine," she mumbled as she picked up the crystal glass and raised it to her nose and sniffed. "It smells dreadful." She put the glass to her lips and took a tentative sip. "It tastes worse than it smells. How is that possible?" She slid the glass back across his desk. "You finish it."

"Don't mind if I do." He tossed back the contents, let out a sigh, and relaxed in his chair.

Elizabeth inhaled and exhaled, trying to get her temper under control. Which, of course, battled against embarrassment. Embarrassment that her brother knew she'd given her virginity to Amesbury. She refused to think of him as Edward. Refused to think of her brother thinking of her having sexual relations with Amesbury. She wasn't successful in not thinking about it and heat infused her cheeks. "I cannot believe he told you. You do know he did only so you'd make me marry him?"

"Yes, I realize that. But I might add, you were a willing participant in this." He paused, his face draining of color. "You were willing, were you not? He didn't...?"

Spencer's words caused her to gasp. "Of course I was willing. Don't be ridiculous, Amesbury would never..."

"Good." Her brother exhaled. "For a moment, I panicked. Thinking of Miranda's history has my mind dredge up horrible scenarios sometimes. Anyway," his arm swept out, "I'd rather not discuss the particulars. He compromised you, ruined you for another, and you could be carrying his child. He is procuring a special license as we speak. The nuptials will take place in two days. Then you will spend your honeymoon at Cliff House. Don't look so shocked, you knew this could happen? He loves you. Let him explain with his own words about his past. I beg of you to give him a chance and I never beg."

"Why?" Tears leaked from her eyes, and she swiped them away in disgust.

"Because I saw you two together. Your eyes lit up every time he entered a room. Love shined from them. Also from his. You would regret this for the rest of your life. Take it from someone who knows what it is like to love and lose that person." His hand combed through his hair. "Yes, Miranda and I are together now, but for ten years my life was torture."

"You hid it well."

"Yes I did. Would you want to hide your broken heart for life?"

Would she? The beat of her heart thumped against her chest in a fast, steady rhythm. The answer was no. That didn't mean she forgave Amesbury for his sins and for hiding his past. She would not just fall into his arms and profess her love. No. He would have to earn it back. Giving it freely would not happen until Elizabeth came to terms with...her stomach ached at thinking about what he'd done. Inhaling, she replied on her exhale, "No. I still love him." Damn the tears silently slipping down her face. "But when I envision him..." Her head shook. "I can't talk about it. Can't speak the words out loud. It will take time for my mind to merge with my heart. I can't promise anything. I will marry him. Willingly go on our honeymoon, but other than that I can't promise anything."

"Thank you." He reached across the desk and squeezed her hand. "I wish the circumstances were different."

She whispered as she left her brother's study, "Me too." Outside in the hall, she leaned her back against the closed door, her arms wrapped around her waist, and she waited for her tears to dry up. It took some time, but the tears eventually stopped and she made her way to her chamber. Her room for a short time only. Because, in two days' time she would become Lady Amesbury and live in Spencer House no more. Elizabeth didn't even know where Amesbury's home in London was. Would it be warm and cozy like here? Or cold and dark and frightening? Her insides unwound as she knew, without really knowing, that his home would be warm and cozy like his country estate.

WAITING PATIENTLY in Lady Silverton's drawing room for

her to receive him had Edward glaring out the windows at the gray clouds promising rain by day's end.

"Lord Amesbury, what a pleasant surprise."

Manners ingrained in him had him bowing. His features, however, were stoic and his eyes glared daggers at her. "Lady Silverton. Thank you for receiving me. May I get right to the point of my visit?"

"Please sit." Her steady hand indicated a hard-back chair, no doubt its only purpose in the room was for unwanted guests. Did she have no shame? He sat, ignoring the ache in his leg and spine with the impending rain.

"Thank you. I think you know why I've come to call. You will not get a shilling from me, never mind ten thousand pounds. While my reputation will be ruined for a time, yours will be ruined for life. Don't make me do something both of us will regret."

She had the decency to blush and gasp, admitting to all he needed to know. Standing, he looked down at her. "While I sympathize with your financial difficulties, you must find another solution. And lest you think to blackmail another visitor to the Red Poppy, I've taken the liberty of notifying all members of your deceit. Good day."

Descending the exterior stairs, he found his steps light and his pain receding. Perhaps the tension and worry had added to his daily aches and pains. He found himself smiling as he alighted his barouche and made way to procure his special license.

THE MORNING of her wedding found Elizabeth dressed in her chemise and stays sitting at her dressing table as Sophie used her skills to tame her hair into an elaborate coiffure. If she used the hot iron another time her maid was liable to burn her hair beyond repair.

"Please, miss, I'm almost done. If you could sit for a moment longer."

What Sophie didn't say was sit still. Her body wanted out of the chair. Nervous energy coiled throughout her, and she needed to pace to rid herself of it. *Inhale, exhale. A few more minutes. I can do this. I can face my marriage.*

When her maid finished and she looked into the glass, she gasped. Her hair had never looked lovelier in a high upsweep with soft curls cascading down around her face and back. Exquisite, soft and feminine. Oh so feminine.

"My dear sister, you look beautiful." Mary exclaimed as she entered the bed chamber.

"Mary," Elizabeth cried as she stood and rushed to hug her sister, mindful of her hair. "I've missed you. Let me look at you." Mary's cheeks were rosy and she looked happy. "Marriage agrees with you."

They chatted as Sophie dressed her in a stunning silk, cream dress. High waist, scooped neckline, puffed short sleeves. The silk skirt pooled softly to the floor. Seed pearls, ribbon, and lace accentuated the neckline, the hem, and the edge of her sleeves. Simple but stunning. Long cream gloves and a crown of blue and white flowers, seed pearls, ribbon, and a long train of delicate lace completed her ensemble.

"You look lovely, my dear." Miranda said as she entered the room. "The cream dress with your dark hair and fair skin is absolutely stunning. Amesbury will not be able to take his eyes of you. We must leave now though. Your chariot awaits."

After her maid wrapped her in a cream, fur trimmed cloak, Elizabeth hesitated, her feet stuck to the floor as reality set in. Today she would marry Amesbury. Her once-upon-a-time dream come true. Her real life prince, or he used to be. *Will I get my happily-ever-after?*

"Elizabeth?" Mary asked, concern etched in her voice and on her face.

Mary must think her silly to be hesitating in marrying Amesbury since she did not know about the issues from his past plaguing their future. "I'm ready." Ready as she would ever be.

Two carriages carried their family to St. Georges in Hanover Square. Grandmother, Mother, Mary and Smythe in one and Spencer, Miranda and her in another.

Her brother took her hand. "I hope you know I would not force you into this marriage if I didn't truly believe it is what you want."

"I know."

"Amesbury is a good man. He will treat you well. He loves you."

"I know."

"Do not be sad."

"I'm not."

Silence followed the rest of the journey to the church. Elizabeth was thankful it would be a small private affair. The last thing she wanted was for the whole of the *ton* turning out to watch her today.

"We have arrived." Her brother's voice broke her out of her thoughts."

Spencer helped, first his wife then her alight from the carriage. Elizabeth ascended the church steps on his arm and once inside, Miranda helped her remove her cloak. They waited until Miranda took her seat, then the violinist started and her brother escorted her up the aisle. Forcing herself not to look at the ground, Elizabeth tilted her head up and gasped as her eyes locked with Amesbury's. Even at this distance she could see he appeared nervous. His smile tight, not natural. He dressed in black formal wear, including hose, black heeled shoes with silver buckles. He looked handsome, but not his usual self. She knew he preferred less formal clothing. If her memory served her correctly, she'd never seen him in hose and shoes. He usually wore breeches and Hessians. That he dressed in appropriate formal attire touched her.

Spencer removed her hand from his arm and placed it on Amesbury's. For one second she saw relief on Amesbury's face and a genuine smile before they turned to face the clergyman. Their vows were spoken in a haze of a dream. When he slipped his ring on Elizabeth's finger tears threatened to escape her eyes. The band of diamonds, one large round one, flanked by smaller ones on either side took her breath away. How had he known she favored diamonds? Had this belonged to his mother?

Amesbury brushed her lips softly when they were joined in holy matrimony. Cheers surrounded them as they made their way down the aisle, out the door, down the stairs, and into Amesbury's carriage for the ride back to Spencer House for the wedding breakfast.

Silence surrounded her in the carriage as she sat next to her new husband—the vacancy of noise near deafening to her ears. Who knew lack of sound could do that?

"May I say you look beautiful today?"

Elizabeth pulled the lap blanket tighter around her. A chill had set in, and she'd left her cape with her sister-in-law.

"You are cold. Let me warm you."

His arms circled her waist, and he moved closer so their bodies touched from feet to shoulder. If she didn't remember what tore them apart, she would rest her head on his shoulder and revel in the closeness and warmth of his body. Enjoy the woodsy sent of his cologne, soft not overbearing. Let the sound of his even breathing lull her. Too bad her mind refused let her forget. Her heart, though, ached for him. Beat for him, was cracked wide open and vulnerable to him.

"Better?"

"Yes. Thank you." Such politeness. Would their marriage be like that? She knew many whose were. She would go insane.

The carriage came to a stop. They had arrived. Her stomach sank. She didn't know if she would survive the wedding breakfast with all eyes on her and her husband. Amesbury helped her out of the coach, tucked her arm into his as they climbed the stone steps, a doorman opened the door and bowed as they entered. Voices could be heard down the hall in the drawing room. They made their way there to find all Elizabeth's family members and most of their friends in attendance, laughing and looking merry as they enjoyed refreshments while awaiting the wedding feast. Champagne flowed freely. Amesbury plucked two flutes off a tray from a passing servant and turned to face her, looking uncomfortable.

"To you, my dear wife, on our wedding day. I will forever be your most humble admirer and loyal servant."

His glass clinked with hers, and as they sipped from the crystal, the other occupants of the room cheered and clinked their flutes.

Before Elizabeth had a chance to say anything back to her husband, they were surrounded by family and friends, everyone talking at once and congratulating them with hugs and kisses. Tears stung her eyes as she moved from one to another—their words a jumble inside her head as she realized all these people loved her and Amesbury. They were truly happy for them. And she was not the only person with tears in her eyes.

When her cousin, the Earl of Bridgeton, pulled her into his arms he said, "There is no better man than Amesbury. I am so happy for you and for him. He has a prize in you, and I'm not just saying that because you're my cousin. I know you are experiencing some difficulties, but I know in my heart they will resolve quickly. One only has to look at you both to know your love for each other runs deep. I love you and I'm the proudest cousin alive today."

"You are making me cry." He stepped back and handed her his handkerchief. "Thank you." She dabbed at her eyes and nose. "May I keep this?"

"Of course. But I hope for only happy tears."

"Me too." And she found herself relaxing. Perhaps today wouldn't be so awful.

For three quarters of an hour Elizabeth spent time conversing with all her friends and family, alternating between crying and laughing. Her discussion with her mother was most touching.

They went to a quiet corner of the room, sat in two chairs side by side, and she waited for her mother, who looked lovely today in light blue. Her cheeks had color. It was a good day for her. Elizabeth worried about her so much. Had ever since she was a little girl and realized her mother seldom left her room and was as fragile as the most delicate china.

"My dear Elizabeth," Mother spoke softly, taking one of her hands in her cool one. "Please forgive me for not visiting your room last evening for the mother, daughter wedding night talk." Her poor mother sounded guilty. "Is there anything you wish to ask me?"

Since her husband had already bedded her, she had nothing to ask. Although she couldn't let her mother know she was no longer innocent. "There is nothing to forgive. Miranda kindly explained things to me." She forced herself to blush.

"She is a wonderful daughter-in-law and sister-in-law to you and Mary."

Elizabeth squeezed her mother's hand very gently. She was always afraid her mother would break if she hugged her or squeezed her too tightly. "I will miss you. I know I won't live far away, but I worry for you."

A smile graced her mother's face, making her look years younger and more beautiful than ever. "I believe it is a mother's duty to worry over her children. However, my three children have married well. I have no doubt you will be happy with Amesbury. Since he has no family left, I believe we will see the two of you often. Now, I've kept you from your gentleman long enough. I love you daughter, be happy."

Where had she put Bridgeton's handkerchief. Drat, she'd left it on a table across the room. In her entire life, she'd never had a conversation this extensive with her mother. Perhaps her health was improving.

As she made her way to her handkerchief, the butler announced, "Breakfast is served."

Immediately, Amesbury stood at her side offering his arm. The talk with her mother had flustered her, and it took her a moment to wrap her arm around his. "Thank you."

They were at one side of the table, with Spencer and Miranda seated at each end. Mary and Mr. Smythe sat across from the newlyweds. Every other vacant seat was taken with the rest of their family and friends. The footmen began serving everything from coddled eggs, sausages, bacon, fish, fruit, and numerous delicious looking pastries. Elizabeth couldn't possibly eat the contents of her plate with her insides vibrating with nerves.

Several hours later when Amesbury escorted Elizabeth from her family home, she smiled when her eyes fell on Amesbury's carriage decorated with white paper streamers and flowers. Once inside, he pulled up the lap blanket to cover her and tapped the roof of the coach, letting his driver know to move on.

"It is odd that I don't know where you live. How no one

has ever pointed it out to me on one of our strolls to the park, or that I have never visited."

"Not at all since it isn't proper for an unmarried lady to visit a single gentleman. If I entertained perhaps you would have visited. Too relieve your fears that I live in some unfashionable area, I live in Mayfair on Brook Street, not so far from Spencer House."

"All I want is to be close to my family." That he thought she would care if they lived outside Mayfair bothered her. Her sister lived outside of Mayfair and it didn't bother Mary. If they lived near Mary she wouldn't mind. Elizabeth never put on airs. At one point she had wanted to move to America and see the Wild West. Most ladies in London drawing rooms would swoon at the thought. Not her. Perhaps someday Amesbury would take her to America for holiday.

The carriage stopped and as she exited she gasped as she got her first glimpse of her new home. Four stories of white stone and beautiful large mullion windows. The ground floor windows were decorated with flower boxes filled to the brim with an explosion of color. A sizable portico welcomed her to the entrance and drew her toward the wood and leaded glass, black front door.

"It is beautiful, graceful, and not what I'd expected."

His brow quirked as he grinned at her. "No. And why is that, my dear?"

"For one, my lord, I kept thinking about manly houses. Built for single gentlemen in dark brick and hard lines. But I shouldn't have been surprised as this has been in your family for generations. I presume anyway."

He chuckled as he escorted her into the main entry, which was two stories high with marble floors and a marble staircase that curved gracefully up to the second story. "You will find this house more feminine than masculine. My mother had the home redone shortly before her death. It's a pity she didn't get to enjoy the beauty of her designs for long."

"She designed this?"

"She worked tirelessly with the carpenters, wanting to add her touch to the entire home." He paused and cleared his throat. "Which she did. If something is not to your liking, please let me know and I will hire workers to change things."

Elizabeth gasped. "No, if the rest of the home is like the entryway, it is perfect. I wouldn't change a thing." Out of the corner of her eye, relief washed across her new husband's face. How could she change anything when this home represented the family he lost?

HEARING her address him as 'my lord' had Edward's insides churning. He hadn't realized, although he should have, that it would take time to win Elizabeth over to the carefree way their relationship used to be. In fact, since he'd made her acquaintance, he didn't think she'd ever referred him as my lord, always Amesbury or Edward. "Please call me Edward. We are married now. Can we drop the formality between us?"

When she finally answered, she didn't meet his eyes. "Yes. Edward. May I see our rooms? I believe my maid, who would have arrived hours ago, should be done unpacking my things."

"By all means."

Up the grand staircase and to the left were their chambers. He opened the door to her rooms first.

EYES WIDE, Elizabeth took in her exquisite surroundings. Edward's mother had outdone herself in the marchioness's rooms. A palette of soft blue, pink, and cream was prominent throughout the rooms consisting of a sitting room, bedroom, and dressing room with a separate bathing chamber as well. She would be happy here.

"You haven't said anything. Are these rooms to your liking?"

"Oh yes. They are lovely and very comfortable looking."

"Good." He swept his hand out, indicating a door off her sitting room. "My rooms are this way. Please follow me."

Obediently, Elizabeth followed him as her stomach fluttered to be seeing his rooms, knowing they were married and it wouldn't be scandalous. They mirrored hers in that they entered his sitting room. His mother must have spent much time in here because her design touches stood out all around. Deep blue, brown, and cream made up the sitting room. The furniture was larger and more masculine, though subtle decorative pieces softened the room. They bypassed his dressing room and bathing chamber and stepped into his bedroom. A massive four poster bed took up the center of the room with deep blue velvet hangings. The floors, like hers, were wood but covered with expensive, thick rugs from the orient. No expense was spared in the interior of Worthington House.

"My mother was planning on redoing Cliff House when the accident happened. Perhaps when next we are there you may wish to make changes."

"Milord." Edward's valet bowed. "Milady. I have two footmen ready to move your belongings to your new rooms."

"Send them now. We are done here."

"Thank you, milord." He bowed and left.

"You don't use these rooms?"

At her query Edward winced. "No. After my parent's death I remained in my old rooms. I didn't want to move here until I married and had my marchioness." Without another word he exited through the adjourning room. "I would think you'd like to rest before dinner, which is served promptly at seventy-thirty." He bowed. "Until then."

What? He just left as if she were a guest and not his wife. And then she recalled his wince when she inquired about now using the marquess's rooms. Poor Edward, he'd never recovered from losing his family. Would their marriage help him accept and move forward? She said a quick prayer that it did. Even in her anger with him, she loved him so much her heart ached.

She made her way to the lovely blue and pink damask chaise lounge and got comfortable. Napping would not happen as she wasn't tired, but she hoped enjoying some peace in front of the blazing hearth would soothe her spirits and worry. Except tears filled her eyes. Ever since Elizabeth had been a little girl she'd dreamed of her wedding day. The horses, their necks adorned with wreaths of pink and white roses pulling an open carriage. Inside the carriage rose petals covered every conceivable surface. And her new husband lavished his attentions on her.

Never, in her wildest dreams, had she expected her husband to treat her so callously. More tears fell and Elizabeth hated herself for them. For the past year she'd wanted to marry Edward. Loved him. She'd gotten her wish. So why did excruciating pain radiate inside her chest? Happiness should be surrounding them in its fold. Not this gloom and doom hovering over them like a massive storm threatening destruction to everything in its path. If only Elizabeth could go back to the night of the masquerade and never overhear the conversation that changed her opinion of Edward. He'd tried to explain, but she'd been so cross and hurt she'd barely heard his explanation. Their marriage would remain trapped beneath the storm clouds unless she insisted on him telling all that happened once he buried his family. Somehow she didn't think it would be easy. A more private person she'd never known.

"Milady," Sophie said as she entered the room. "It is time to dress for dinner." Elizabeth sat up and stretched her arms and back. Evidently she'd been tired because she had dosed off.

CHAPTER FIFTEEN

SITTING IN HIS STUDY, CRADLING A GLASS WITH TWO fingers of brandy in it, Edward swore at himself. *I treated her abominably. She must hate me.*

When Edward had left her in her rooms, more like dismissed her, the shock and hurt on her face had flashed in his eyes. What an arse he was. Elizabeth, who radiated kindness, happiness, and loyalty deserved more than him. He, with his broken body, heart, and soul. Oh, for a time he'd thought she'd healed him, but it didn't take long for his demons to take root again. And now, thanks to him, Elizabeth would live out her entire life surrounded by him and his demons.

Today had physically exhausted his body. If Edward could make it through dinner without his cane, miracles could happen, which, of course, he needed. On their first day of marriage he didn't want to frighten Elizabeth by using his cane in front of her. He didn't want her to think she'd wed a cripple. Although, in reality, she had. Or Edward would be a cripple eventually as day by day, month by month his back and legs progressively worsened. By forty, he'd be reduced to using a chair with wheels like an old, decrepit invalid.

A vice clamped around Edward's insides which caused him to gasp. Who knew guilt caused such physical pain. He should've been upfront with his weaknesses—emotional and physical. No one had called him out on it. He was surprised Wentworth and Myles hadn't realized he seldom rode anymore. His days of racing through Hyde Park were ancient history.

The sound of the dinner bell warning shocked him out of his maudlin. He had half an hour to make himself presentable for his new bride.

In Edward's chambers all appeared silent next door, and he wondered if Elizabeth had already made her way downstairs and he'd missed her on the main staircase. Then suddenly voices and several pairs of feet moved around next door. His valet appeared at his side, giving him a start.

"You appear in pain, may I get your cane, milord?"

"Hell, no. Just help me dress for dinner."

"There has been a change in plans. Mrs. Potter has ordered dinner to be served in milady's sitting room."

He was going to fire his housekeeper. "On whose orders?" he barked. "Never mind. I'll deal with Mrs. Potter later. You may go, Gerard."

"But you said..."

"I know what I said, but since I'm dining casually, what I'm wearing is suitable."

"Yes, milord," Gerard said and left with a bow.

In fact, he removed his coat. It was damn stifling inside his rooms. His shirtsleeves and waistcoat would have to do. If he planned on seducing his wife, he would change into his robe, if only...

Mrs. Potter knew what she was doing. Between her, Gerard, and his butler, Stephens, they were always poking into his affairs ever since the accident. More since his struggle with opium. They were the only three in his employ that knew. And they were loyal. Damn it, Edward couldn't be angry at Mrs. Potter. The three of them were like family. How he wished to make a family with Elizabeth. He hated to admit his jealousy toward Wentworth, Myles, Bridgeton, and Spencer for the contentment and happiness they lived with daily. Could contentment and happiness be attainable for Elizabeth and him as well? Only time would tell, and time ticked on the longer he stayed in his rooms and avoided hers.

His knuckles wrapped lightly on the adjoining wooden door. He sucked air into his lungs as he waited for a sign to enter. The door opened, and Edward inhaled deeply to make up for not breathing while he'd waited for the door to be answered. He could lie to himself and say that was the cause of his breathlessness, when in fact it was Elizabeth standing before him. Edward's eyes ran from her bare feet peeking out beneath the white robe, up to her waist, bypassing the apex of her thighs, higher to where if he squinted he could make out the darkness of her nipples then on to her face. Heat charged through his body, he undid his cravat and opened the top of his shirt, trying to breathe. Then he looked at his wife's lovely face, her pink cheeks. Thick, wavy chestnut hair cascaded loose to her waist. He fought like hell not to adjust his cock inside his breeches. Not to mention pulling her into his arms and burying himself in her scented hair.

"Please come in." Stepping aside, she curtsied. "I hope this evening finds you well, Edward?"

"Yes and you?"

"Quite well, thank you." Elizabeth's eyes fluttered toward the small table set with covered dishes and champagne flutes with an open bottle breathing in a bucket of ice. "Mrs. Potter insisted we dine in private. I hope you don't mind."

"Not at all." Bloody hell, Edward didn't want to consume

food, only Elizabeth. Was he wrong in thinking she didn't want him? Dare he hope by the way she was dressed, or rather un-dressed?

He helped her into a chair, and as he sat down he realized he'd not been wrong. The glare she sent him showed her anger quite clearly. Instant knot inside his stomach.

"Champagne?" Holding up the bottle he waited for her reply.

"Yes, please," Elizabeth said politely, too politely. Edward hated this game. What he wouldn't do to go back to their carefree relationship they'd once had.

After filling both glasses, he sat back and drained his, forcing himself not to cough as the bubbles filled his throat and nose.

"May I serve you?" Elizabeth opened a covered dish and paused.

"That would be nice, thank you."

He couldn't for the life of him know the contents of the dishes. He ate, but tasted nothing. The sight of her taking little bites here and there between her lush pink lips mesmerized Edward. Since when had eating become an erotic experience? Edward swallowed groan after groan and damn if his cock wasn't peeking out the top of his breeches. He'd long since unbuttoned his waist coat and untucked his shirt. Pushing his stiff member back inside his breeches, he swore when his finger came in contact with some discharge. If he sat here in her presence much longer he'd embarrass himself by coming inside his clothes.

"I believe there is desert and sherry by the hearth." Elizabeth met his eyes with an apologetic smile.

Did she think his time with her was something she needed to apologize for? He wanted her beyond reason. Nothing would happen, though, until she wanted him back.

Before he could make his way around the table, she stood

and strolled in the direction of the fireplace and took a seat on a chaise, leaving a matching chair for him.

REMOVING the metal cover from a dish, Elizabeth hoped Edward didn't notice the quivering of her hand. Oh great! Strawberries and clotted cream. A favorite of hers, but she'd restrain. Eating dinner had unsettled her to no end. Edward had eyed her the entire time over his crystal flute with hunger in his eyes. Hunger for her, not food. He'd practically undressed at the table, and once she could've sworn he reached down to do something. Heat sufficed her cheeks at the thought he'd touched himself. If any more moisture pooled between her thighs, it would soak her night rail and dressing robe. How embarrassing.

She was thankful she was no longer a virgin, as it had her better prepared for this night. Something she didn't need to be frightened of. Only of losing her heart to her husband... again. Something Elizabeth didn't think she'd survive a second time. Giving her heart and then having it ripped from her chest upon learning something nefarious from his past again would crush her. Feeling chilled, she pulled a blanket over her body up to her chest and settled her eyes on her handsome husband's profile. Something appeared to be ruminating around in his mind. Something causing him distress. Was she the cause of his stress?

"You appear preoccupied this evening, Edward. Are you not pleased with our union?"

"Forgive me." He turned his head to meet her eyes. "There is much on my mind."

His hazel eyes swirled with so many emotions, pain, regret, and a touch of guilt. They were both miserable. Miserable with sexual awareness, longing, and how to forgive and move on. At least she struggled with the forgive and move on part. Nothing would please her more than to go and sit on Edward's lap, curl into his body and love him. Damn her pride. Not just stubborn pride, her heart shuddered—fear. She was afraid of rejection.

"There is nothing to forgive," Elizabeth said past the lump in her throat. "Perhaps you will have a better day tomorrow."

"Yes. Perhaps." He rose to his feet slowly, wincing, and nodded his head. "I will leave you to your rest."

I will leave you to your rest. Was he daft? There would be no rest tonight. Sitting up, she took a large berry, dipped it in cream and ate it with great relish then licked her fingers in a most unladylike fashion afterwards. Why not, no one could see her. Elizabeth ate another and another until she removed her robe and climbed beneath the counterpane. Lying on her back with her arms outside the covers she huffed, to keyed up to sleep. This was her wedding night. Her one and only wedding night and she lay in bed alone. Abruptly, she rolled onto her side, hugged her stomach, and sobbed into her pillow.

THE LOW BLAZE in the hearth in the library caused shadows to bounce off the paneled walls. Edward enjoyed the solitude and darkness. He rested in a large comfortable chair, his bare feet on an ottoman, not that he could feel them, they'd gone numb an hour ago. A nightly and sometimes daily occurrence. A brandy snifter cradled between his thumb and forefinger. His mouth twisted up into a grin. He couldn't believe during dinner he'd thought about swiping the food off the table and taking his lovely Elizabeth right there. Too bad he hadn't acted on his impulses.

They would be in bed wrapped in each other's arms now. Warm, naked body against warm, naked body. He was an idiot who deserved to be in Bedlam for the way he'd left her—lounging, looking angelic in white.

His heart? That entity of its own needed her heart for his to survive. He had so much to atone for he didn't know where to start. He should go to her now. Tell her how much he loved her, needed her, and couldn't live without her. Beg her forgiveness for his past transgressions and anything he may do in the future. Put his heart and soul in her hands and pray she didn't crush them.

The pitter-patter of soft footsteps near the doorway alerted Edward that he was no longer alone. "Is someone there?"

The voice of his beloved called out softly, "Yes." Her voice all breathy soothed him instantly.

"Please, join me by the fire."

Softly, on bare feet, she took the identical chair next to his, separated by a small table. He reached for the throw blanket on the back of his chair and handed it to her. Damn, he should stand and cover her himself, but he didn't trust his legs to support his weight and his cane was leaning on the settee out of his reach. Poor place for it.

"Could you not sleep?" he inquired—his voice resonating deeper than he'd expected.

"No. I thought I would find a book to read. I usually read at bedtime. It helps my body and mind relax so I can sleep."

"I know what you mean. I do the same thing." Edward held up the book of poems on the side table. "It didn't keep my interest tonight."

"Do you usually read in here and not in your room?"

"Yes. And if I fall asleep, all the better as I prefer to sleep in a chair. Or at least propped up with numerous pillows in bed."

"Isn't it awkward?"

"No to me." Perhaps he shouldn't have said anything. She might ask more questions. He knew he needed to confide in her, but the truth was, he was afraid. Afraid she might leave him when she learned the truth about him.

"Why don't you pick out a book and I'll escort you back to your room."

A quarter hour later, after Elizabeth had inspected numerous books, she gasped and plucked one off a middle shelf. A shelf that held his mother's gothic novels. Turning she hugged it to her chest and smiled. "This is my favorite book. *The Mysteries of Udolpho* by Ann Radcliffe."

His pulse spiked. "It was my mother's favorite as well. I think you will see how many times she read it by the wearing of the spine.

"Oh, would you like me to pick something else?"

"No," he said quickly. "My mother would've been honored to know my bride had things in common with her." Sadness crept into his voice. It couldn't be helped.

Draining his glass, he placed it on the table. Using the palm of his hands, he smacked his thighs and calves, trying to force feeling back into his legs so he could stand. It was regrettable Elizabeth would see, but he could hardly escort her to her rooms without feeling in his legs.

Elizabeth's eyes widened as she hurried to his side. "What are you doing? You're going to injure yourself."

Ignoring her, he stood and willed his legs to move. Torturously, he moved one step at a time toward his cane. *Nearly there...three more steps...two.* As if in slow motion and without any control at all, his legs buckled and his body crashed to the ground—half landing on the settee and half on the carpet.

"Edward," Elizabeth screamed and dropped to the ground beside him. She looked positively aghast as she grabbed his arm and helped him to sit. "What happened?"

"Milord?" Gerard's voice came from the opened doors. "Do you need assistance?"

"No. I'm fine." No matter how many times he told Gerard or Stephens—who took turns watching out for him—to go to bed, they hovered around him at night. Their loyalty and concern touched him, and his throat burned.

"Goodnight then, milord, milady."

ELIZABETH COULDN'T BREATHE. Seeing Edward collapse took decades off her life. Ever since Elizabeth had entered the library he'd acted stranger than usual. When he began beating his legs she didn't know what to think. Had he gone mad? Was he drunk? He hadn't acted or sounded in his cups.

Sitting next to him now, listening to his heavy breathing, frightened her. He started punching his thighs, she grabbed one of his hands and said, "Please, you are frightening me."

"I'm sorry. I don't mean to."

"Please stop that."

His other hand stilled and he settled against the back of the settee.

"Talk to me please." Her heart pounded, tears clogged her throat and stung her eyes. Without thinking of anything but his comfort and safety, Elizabeth wrapped one arm through Edward's and snuggled close to his side, her head resting against his shoulder. Her other hand rested on his chest, covering his heart. After a time, the erratic beat of his heart seemed to calm and his breathing evened out.

"I'm sorry." He turned his head and pressed a kiss to the top of her head.

Tears trickled down Elizabeth's cheeks, and she didn't bother to wipe them away. When they pooled on her lashes, she blinked, forcing them down her cheeks and her vision cleared. At least until it started all over again.

"There are still things you don't know about what happened to me after the accident." He rubbed the top of her head with his cheek. "I explained to you how I broke my back and struggled for many months to learn to walk again. What I neglected to tell you was that due to the injury to my spine, my condition is getting worse. Ever since the accident, I get severe pain in my lower back and down the outside of my legs—like a blade sliding up and down my leg. After, numbness sets in, and I must sit or lie down for long periods of time."

"But...how have you hidden this?"

Exhaling, he continued. "It was difficult. Whenever I'm home I use a cane. I never socialized all that much unless I accompanied Wentworth or Myles. They know I use a cane when in the privacy of my home, but even they do not know how desperate I've become. I have exercise equipment in my old rooms that help to strengthen my back and legs. It appears to not be working very well anymore. Anyway, lately the pain and numbness have been progressing. I've been unfair to you. I should've told you. I will understand if you want an annulment."

She gasped, rose up on her knees on the settee, and got close to his face with hers. "There will be no annulment. I'm your wife, your marchioness, and I'm not going anywhere. You are stuck with me. Besides, my brother would never let me back inside the house. He was so thankful someone was willing to marry me. You will not get rid of me. We will deal with this. Find a specialist. When was the last time you saw one?

"Last week. He told me the same thing he always does. Strengthen my back, use the cane, take laudanum for pain.

Fight through the numbness and get rest. He also said perhaps it is time for a chair with wheels.

A sob escaped Elizabeth's mouth before she could stifle it behind her hand. Edward's eyes widened, and with a horrified expression, he pushed her aside and stood with his cane this time and made his way toward the door.

"Wait," she cried. "Wait."

CHAPTER SIXTEEN

WAIT. EDWARD WOULD WAIT AN ETERNITY FOR HER IF only he were whole. Enough of that. He scolded himself as he heard soft footsteps draw near his side as he approached the marble staircase.

"May I help you?"

Before he could answer she wrapped her arm around his free one. The one meant for the bannister. He allowed it and with a fair amount of discomfort they ascended the stairs and made their way to her chamber door.

"Please, will you join me? There are things we still need to discuss," Elizabeth said softly.

Waiting for his response, she moved to her bed and piled pillows against the headboard for his comfort and hers. "Do you need assistance?"

"Christ no," he scoffed and climbed on the bed, leaning against the pillows and sighing. Damn it felt good to be in bed. His eyes found Elizabeth's, and his heart dropped at the look of uncertainty on her face. He padded the space beside him. "Join me."

Instead of sitting on the covers as he had, she climbed

beneath them but rested her head on the same pillow as his, awaking his lust.

"Can you explain things to me now?" More soft spoken words from his wife. But he knew, even though they were spoken in a question, she wanted answers and she wanted them tonight.

However, instant pain jabbed his scull whenever he thought about his past. Elizabeth deserved to know everything. And once she heard all, she could make the decision to forgive him and be his wife or not. The choice was hers and hers alone to make.

"For years I used laudanum for the pain after the carriage accident. I didn't abuse it at first, but it didn't take long to build up a tolerance for it. Because the affects were slight on me, I could dose myself and go out to a ball or one of my clubs or even riding in Hyde Park and no one knew." He took her hand and laced their fingers together—hers soft and warm, his hard and cool.

"Right after I became betrothed to Lady Beth, which proved a disaster from the start..."

"May I interrupt?"

"Yes."

"I've always wondered why you asked her to marry you and how it ended without much scandal to either of you?"

Great. Another chapter in his life that embarrassed him. "You have to understand, Wentworth and Myles had traveled to America and left me alone. I know what you're thinking, that I'm a grown man, I can be alone. Well, they'd watched over me since my family's death, and I'd become part of both their families. I didn't know how to be alone. Something I learned quickly though. One night I think I dosed too much laudanum and found myself out on a terrace with Lady Beth after dancing a set with her. Something came over me, and I blurted out a marriage proposal. I was shocked beyond words when she answered yes."

"She is lovely."

"Is she? I hardly noticed. It doesn't matter now since she is married to an American and living in Boston. Happily, I hope. She deserves it for what I put her through. Anyway, that same night I was taking a dose in a dark hallway and a couple stumbled upon me. Before I could work up mortification, they noticed the vile and invited me to a private party..."

"The Red Poppy," Elizabeth interjected.

"Yes. There are others, but the Red Poppy caters mostly to the higher classes. I went. Got turned on to opium, a purer form of laudanum. That first night I sat in a chair and watched, drugged out of my mind, but I knew it was a den of iniquity. People left propriety and morals at the door."

Elizabeth squeezed his hand. "I still cannot believe places like that exist for people of the *ton*. Every time I attend a function I'm going to be looking around wondering."

"For the most part, you will never guess correctly." He sighed in disgust at himself. "Would anyone think it of me?"

"No."

"There is your answer."

"Will you tell me who attends?" she asked.

"No. Knowing will do you no good. Hypothetically, let's say one of Myles's sisters is being courted by a gentleman I know to attend, I would have a private word with Myles. He would need to know, but you, my dear, do not. Not unless some fool pays too much attention to you. In no uncertain terms would I allow such a thing. Nor would I allow it, if you became quite friendly with a lady who belonged. We are getting off topic."

"Please continue."

"At an opium den, people lose their morals, their inhibitions and their clothing. I regret to say I experimented with orgies." His insides stilled at hearing Elizabeth gasp. Edward swallowed loudly and forged on. "If you think other men were involved, let me tell you now they were not. I may have gone to bed with three or four women at once, but I drew the line at men. Thank God parts of my brain still functioned. My involvement lasted perhaps a month before it disgusted me."

"Good."

"So when the lady approached me at the masquerade, we hadn't spoken to each other for nearly two years. Not since the last time I attended the Red Poppy. Actually, I was shocked she remembered me. Drugs and time have a way of making people forget all sorts of things, people and places." He turned so he could look into her eyes. "From the first time I met you, I've been with no one."

"Is there more?" she asked, her voice hesitant and her eyes soft with compassion.

"Yes. I don't believe I ever told you about the time Wentworth and Myles saved me. One night I took too much. Stephens found me in my study unconscious. He sent for the doctor and for my friends. They helped me withdraw from the drug and kept me alive when I begged for death. Tried to end it."

Her eyes widened with shock and her mouth opened, but no words or sound escaped.

"After two weeks and the help of very watchful friends, I'm the man you see here today. Although to say I was cured after two weeks would be a lie. I struggle with opium and wanting it to this day. But believe me when I say, I will never touch the stuff again as long as I live."

"Thank you for being honest." Elizabeth paused, looking uncertain as to what she wanted to say next. "What about Lady Beth?"

"Oh, yes, I truly didn't know what happened except her father called the betrothal off. It was sometime later that

Wentworth admitted to going to the man and begging him to end it. Wentworth believed the stress of my betrothal had led to my downfall."

"Was it true?"

"No, but it didn't help." He cradled her face in his hands and brushed his thumb across her lips. "Please forgive me for causing you undo pain and anguish. I planned on telling you everything before we wed. But then you overheard..."

"I'm sorry." She removed the covers and rose up on her knees. "I should've had more faith in you. Let you explain. Instead I thought the worst."

He placed one hand on her soft, warm cheek and she leaned into his palm. "We both made mistakes. I swear to you," he placed his hand over his heart, "I swear to God, I will never be that man ever again." They may have solved that problem, but they still had his physical problems to discuss. But for the rest of the night he wanted to love her as she deserved to be loved.

Edward took his time making love to his new bride. Every time he looked at her naked body, flush and beautiful, his heart constricted. Her cheeks rosy, her eyes illuminating with desire and love brought emotions to the surface he never knew existed inside him. For as long as he lived, he would remember this night. The night his wife trusted him with her heart and soul and her future. A future he hoped included children and many, many years of happiness, good health, and love.

"Edward," Elizabeth gasped as he entered her. "I love you. Forever and ever and more."

Burying his face in her neck he murmured, "And I you. Forever and more." Their lips met and Edward kissed her with everything he had inside himself. He gave himself over to her fully. And he was rewarded as she gave herself over to him completely when her body shattered in his arms.

EPILOGUE

THE SPENCER FAMILY SPENT A FORTNIGHT TOGETHER AT
the Spencer Estate in Dover. Elizabeth and Mary's mother
and grandmother attended. Grandmother was getting on in
years, but Mother was blossoming with renewed health,
which pleased Elizabeth to no end. It meant she would be
around for many years to come to enjoy her grandchildren
since all three Spencer ladies were increasing. Miranda was
due first, then Mary and then to Elizabeth's utter happiness,
her.

There were not three prouder men in all of England than
Spencer, Robert, and Edward. One would think having children was something new. Not a blessing that had happened
since the beginning of time. But seeing their men, proud and
happy, made all three women more than ecstatic and excited
to welcome the additions to the family.

After visiting several specialists for Edward's back, he had
improved. Elizabeth thought much of it had to do with his
new outlook on life, easing his guilt from the accident and
the worry of trying to hide so many secrets. His conscience
was eased.

Robert was currently working with the War Office. A job the Duke of Newbury had offered him. He still worked private cases. Thankfully, none of his friends and family needed his services.

Mary loved married life. Perhaps invitations to some of the most prestigious balls in London didn't arrive in her daily mail, but she didn't mind. She had the man she loved, a baby on the way, and the love of her family and friends. What more could a woman want? Although—she did want one thing—for her husband to be safe in his new career. Besides worrying for his safety, life was more filling and complete than she ever thought imaginable. Happily-ever-afters did come true to those who fought for it and never lost hope.

The End

ABOUT THE AUTHOR

Christine Donovan is an International Bestselling Author who writes romance that touches the heart, soothes the soul and feeds the mind. She is a PAN Member of RWA and belongs to Novelist, Inc. and Rhode Island Romance Writers. She lives on the Southeast Coast of Massachusetts with her husband. She has four grown sons, one granddaughter, three cats and one spoiled golden retriever. As well as writing historical romance set in the regency era, she also writes contemporary and paranormal. In her spare time, she can be found at the beach, reading, painting or gardening. She loves to tackle DIY projects. Please visit her at http://www.christinedonovan.org

facebook.com/christine.donovanauthor

twitter.com/home

instagram.com/christinedonovan6

ALSO BY CHRISTINE DONOVAN

A Seabrook Family Saga Series

THE RELUCTANT DUKE

THE LADY AND THE EARL

THE LADY MUST CHOOSE

LORD SEBASTIAN AND THE SCOTTISH LASS

SPENCER MEETS HIS LADY LOVE

A Standish Bay Romance Series

BLACKJACK

BRIDGET

MITCH

A Single Title Contemporary

SUNSET BEACH

A Novella

VENETIAN HOLIDAY

www.ingramcontent.com/pod-product-compliance
Lightning Source LLC
Chambersburg PA
CBHW032140170626
46808CB00006B/2318